Elixir

Book One in the Red Plague Trilogy
By Anna Abner

Jade
It was great to
meet you!

An
Ab

Praise for The Dark Caster Series

"A sizzling and sweet paranormal romance."
5 out of 5 stars.
   --Christine Rains, author of the 13th Floor Series

"A wonderful, suspenseful love story."
5 out of 5 stars.
                              --Coffee Time Romance

"A great paranormal adventure with many twists and turns."
5 out of 5 stars.
                              --Community Bookstop

"This book kept me on the edge of my seat."
4 out of 5 stars.
                              --The Reading Café

"This book is brilliant! ... Fascinating and electrifying with memorable characters." 5 out of 5 stars.
                              --SimpliRead

Books by Anna Abner

Spell of Summoning (Dark Caster Book One)
Spell of Binding (Dark Caster Book Two)
Elixir (Red Plague Trilogy Book One)
Antidote (Red Plague Trilogy Book Two)
Panacea (Red Plague Trilogy Book Three)

Subscribe to Anna's monthly newsletter for sneak peeks, updates, and bonus material!

Happy reading!

Acknowledgements

Thank you to Jaycee DeLorenzo at Sweet and Spicy Designs for her beautiful and creative covers and to Jeff Hill at Driving the Quill for his insightful editing.

Thank you to my beta readers for all your help. Rachel R., Paula R., Mary L., Julie L., Suzanne G., Susan C., and Miechi J. Your comments made my story better, and I can never repay you.

I dedicate this story to my daughter, my shining star.

Chapter One

A buzzing circular saw woke me five minutes before my alarm was supposed to go off. Instant, achy terror consumed me. I scrambled out of bed in my PJs and crouched at the end of the hall, peeking around the corner into the living room beyond the foyer.

"Dad?" I hissed.

He stood, hands on hips, in front of our big screen TV staring at local news.

I sagged against the wall in relief. For a moment I'd thought… But no. We weren't being attacked by red-eyed plague victims.

Dad hadn't heard me, but around and between his arms I watched the agitated news anchor struggle through her report.

"If you are in a heavily infected area," the hollow-eyed brunette read off the teleprompter, "you are instructed to shelter in place. Do not attempt to travel. Roads and highways are impassable, particularly in Raleigh and Charlotte. The safest thing for you to do is stay where you are. Lock your doors and windows and wait for further instruction."

A tiny hiccup of fright escaped my throat, and Dad whipped his head around. His normally slicked back blond hair was dry and messy as if he hadn't bothered to comb it at all.

"Maya," he exclaimed, pasting on a friendly smile. But under the positive facade I could tell he was just as terrified as I was. The world was falling to pieces and we both knew it. "Good morning, baby girl. Did the construction wake you up? I told them not to make noise until after six."

Baby girl. He hadn't called me that in two years. Not since Mom's funeral.

"Dad," I said, twisting my fingers around a long tendril of dark hair. "What is going on?" I had fallen asleep worried about the incredibly fast-moving 212R virus and woken up in a construction zone.

"Oh." He glanced through the kitchen archway toward the saw noises. "These men are building a survival bunker in the pantry. I think I mentioned it last week. It's like a panic room, but it won't require electricity."

"Why do we need that?" Was I not panicking enough? 212R was infecting densely populated urban areas and, after three days of fever, stripping the diseased of their higher level thinking skills and replacing them with insatiable cravings for raw flesh and blood.

Victims were crawling all over the larger cities. We were safe, for the moment, in our suburb. But we might not be for long.

"Don't worry about it," he said, showing me another fake smile, making me even jumpier. "It's an insurance policy. Get dressed and we'll have breakfast."

I slipped into my bedroom and tugged on my track gear—shorts, tee, and cross-trainers—in record time to catch up to Dad and one of the construction workers at the kitchen island.

Dad pulled stacks of wrapped twenties from his shoulder bag and slid them across the granite counter toward the man.

"It's more than I told you," Dad said quietly. "Can you finish before two?"

"No problem, boss." The man glanced at me. "With the four of us working nonstop it'll be done in a couple hours."

"With an independent ventilation system?"

"Exactly like we talked about."

"Sanitation station?"

"Roger's putting in the piping now."

I cleared my throat. "Do you want cereal, Dad? There's some oatmeal left."

He flinched as if he'd forgotten I was there. "Baby girl, make whatever you want. I have to go in a minute."

My belly plummeted. "You're going to work?"

The television, the small one next to the

toaster oven, was tuned to cable news. On the screen was a fuzzy snapshot of an infected man, his face splattered with blood and his eyes a distinct and deep shade of red.

The news anchor said hotly to his guest, "We will not call them the Z word, Professor. They are ill and need our support, not our ridicule." He choked up, covering his mouth for a moment. "My mother has been sick the last couple days. Her eyes went red last night." He inhaled a shaky breath. "I won't stand for that kind of language. Not on this show."

On the right side of the screen was a cautionary graphic with bullet points. Stay indoors. Conserve energy. Boil water and keep it in sealed containers. Phone calls for emergencies only.

"I'm sorry." Dad used the remote to turn off the TV. "You don't need to watch this nonsense. It's all posturing and fear mongering."

Well, they had succeeded. I was terrified. "Should I stay home from school?"

"No," Dad said. "The virus isn't here yet. The best thing for you to do is go to school, see your friends, run track, just be *normal*."

"But the news—"

"It's bad in the cities," he agreed, "but we're not in the city. If 212R is here, it's new. We have time."

Up to three days. That's how long it took the infection to invade a body and take over

---

completely.

"Your lab is in Raleigh," I reminded him. "It's not safe there."

He cupped my face, and though his touch was gentle, his fingers were tense as talons against my cheeks. "A cure exists, Maya, but I have to finish synthesizing the antiserum. If all my staff shows up I can finish it today. *I have to go.*"

I opened my mouth to argue further. He was one chemist toiling in a Center for Disease Control lab full of scientists and technicians. What difference would his absence make, honestly, in the grand scheme?

"I can put an end to this," he said, his voice turning husky with emotion. "I can fix everything. I can *save* them."

I saw in the set of his jaw and the steel in his spine I was not going to convince him to stay.

My stomach unraveled like an old scarf. "But you'll come home tonight?"

"Of course." He backed away, gesturing to the counter by the sink. "On your way to school, will you return Mrs. Kinley's dish? It's been sitting here for a week."

"Okay."

"I'm sorry I'm in such a hurry," he said, collecting his satchel, keys, and cell phone. "The CDC is sending a helicopter to pick me up."

I walked him to the front door, getting that itchy feeling I used to get when he dropped

Mason and I off at day care years ago. I didn't want him to go.

"Don't forget," he said, pausing at the threshold, "wash your hands constantly. Carry sanitizer with you. No shaking hands. No hugs. Eat and drink from sealed containers only."

"I will, Dad." I'd heard his cleanliness rules so often, especially in the last few weeks when 212R was all anybody could talk about, I knew them by heart.

"Come home tonight," I pleaded one last time. Since Mom died and my twin brother Mason went away, Dad was all I had left. "Promise me? No matter how much work you still have to do?"

"I'll come home. And I'll bring a generator for the bunker." He kissed my forehead and drove off in his car.

I had almost forgotten the workers banging away in my kitchen until I shut the front door and came face to face with their crew leader.

"Any little extras you want in there?" he asked, smacking his lips as he studied my hair. "Since your daddy is paying for it. I can throw in carpeting. Would you like that? What about a bulletproof peephole?"

Tucking my hair behind both ears, I edged toward the hallway and my bedroom. "Sounds good. Thanks."

I twisted my hair into a bun, packed a bag with a change of clothes, my copy of

Shakespeare's sonnets for English class, and my school binder. Before leaving my room I hesitated in the doorway staring, unfocused, at my honey colored guitar. Holding it in my arms, strumming the strings, and feeling the chords' vibrations in my ribcage was the best part of my day. But it would be a pain to carry it from class to class so I left it behind, promising myself to play it when I got home.

I left the house in a hurry, snatching the baking dish off the kitchen counter on the way out.

Mrs. Kinley opened her front door, but only after I knocked five or six times. And when she did, her hair usually in a sleek ponytail down the back of her neck laid loose and wild.

"Maya, what are you doing out there?" She yanked me inside, slamming the door and locking it behind me. "Are you watching the news? It isn't safe."

"Have they closed the schools?" Maybe I wouldn't have to go after all, no matter what my dad thought.

"Not here. But they did in Raleigh." Her cat Freckles darted across the room as if she had a ghost on her long fluffy tail. "They're closing down the whole city. This zombie plague is ridiculous."

The Z word, the word we weren't supposed to say.

"Do you know what they just said on TV?"

she added. "Reds can't speak." Her eyes filled with unshed tears, and she reached for my hand. Her fingers were cold, but strong. "Isn't that the saddest thing you've ever heard? Even if they wanted to communicate, they physically can't."

Extricating my hand, I tried to smile reassuringly, but I feared it was more of a sneer. "It's sad."

"The saddest," she said, turning back to the box she was packing on her living room sofa.

"My dad went to work in Raleigh," I said. "He's trying to finish a cure."

"Bless his heart." Her words were kind, but her eyes were resolute as if she'd already written him off. "Do you want to stay here with me until he gets home?"

"I'm going to school," I announced bravely, though I felt anything but. "I just wanted to give this back." I showed her the dish. "Thanks again for the brownies. They were really good."

"My pleasure." She pulled me in for a longer and tighter than normal hug, and I rested my chin on her shoulder. Enveloped in Mrs. Kinley's soft, sweet smelling arms, I missed my mom more than ever. "Be safe. Not even our little corner of the world is immune to all this." She waved her hand toward the living room to encompass the news on the TV.

"I will." Readjusting my backpack I crossed her lawn and slid behind the wheel of my car, a rinky-dink coupe my dad had bought for me to practice on.

Palmetto High School was practically deserted. And it wasn't just students ditching under the threat of plague. Half the teachers were absent and only a handful of subs showed up to cover their classes. Lots of kids crammed into classrooms they wouldn't normally be in.

But my track coach was right on time and ready to sweat.

"I hope you delicate flowers came to work," Coach greeted us. "No bird or pig or, I don't know, *raccoon* flu is going to stop us, right?"

I glanced to my right at the three other runners who'd shown up to morning practice and nodded woodenly.

"That's what I love to see." Coach blew her whistle. "Warm up mile. Let's go, ladies."

I took off, quickly outpacing my teammates.

My best event was the one thousand meter. I was fast on a normal day. Maybe the panic and anxiety helped fuel me because I was better than fast. I was a machine in drills, not even caring about the humid, North Carolina air hanging heavy and thick. As I sprinted sweat blossomed, coating me in sticky moisture, but I never slowed down. By the time the first bell rang I was wrung out. I showered in the locker room and hurried to first period.

My history teacher Mr. Coates had the TV on and nobody even pretended to study or finish assignments. We scooted under the television and absorbed live footage from New York and Miami, the hardest hit U.S cities so far.

And North Carolina was right between them.

Infected plague victims, red eyes seeming to glow, swarmed the streets attacking and consuming people. Survivors jammed all major routes of transportation—freeways, train depots, airports.

"Lola Rodriguez had no way of knowing her first floor apartment would be attacked in the middle of the night by a 212R sufferer," Daniela, a veteran reporter announced to the camera. "Thanks to her quick thinking she not only saved her own life but the lives of three of her neighbors by waking them up and hiding them on a second floor terrace."

They looped a short video clip of a Red climbing a staircase, getting about halfway up, and toppling over like a toy soldier on a shaky table.

"As we've learned in the past few days," the anchor continued, "212R affects the inner ear. Sufferers will not be able to either rise or descend more than a few feet before feeling uncontrollably dizzy."

I glanced at the windows. Red eyes, no speech, and an inability to climb. Oh, and an insatiable craving for raw flesh and blood. And they were out there, not that far away, in Raleigh and Charlotte.

The reporter wrapped up her segment. "If there's one thing to take away from the last hour," Daniela said, "it is to shelter in place. Please, *please,* if you are in any of the major plague centers immediately find a safe spot to be for the next few days." She smiled sadly. "My heart goes out to those suffering, both victims and survivors. If you can hear my voice, stay safe. Stay vigilant. We will get through this."

The show went to commercial at the same time the bell rang, and I nearly jumped out of my skin.

On the way out of the room, even though it was against the rules, I brought my cell out of my bag and texted my dad. "Did you make it to work?"

Seconds ticked by. A minute. I waited in the hall. Just as I was about to put it away and go to my next class I received a text.

"I got to ride in a helicopter! Everything good. Working hard. Are you in school?"

"Yes. I love you."

"Love you too."

The next three classes went about the same as first period. At lunch I did what I always did, slipped into the band room to play guitar with my friend Guinevere. But Gwen wasn't there so I stuck a granola bar in my mouth, pulled a student guitar from its case, and plucked a couple notes.

I played an upbeat country pop song on my

instrument. The kind of song I loved. Normally.

It rang false. Nothing about the world was light and snappy anymore.

The side door slammed open and Cal poked his head in, his cold, calculating eyes discovering me sitting all by myself. The very sight of him caused a sour fear to spike inside my chest.

On any other day there were enough people in the room to create a buffer between Cal and I, but it was just the two of us.

Apparently, not even the threat of infection and death could suppress his sadistic impulses.

"Hey dork." He grinned as he produced a chocolate milk grenade and pretended to bite an invisible pin from the top of the container. "Incoming!"

I abandoned the school's guitar and took off a split second before he threw it overhand, digging my feet into the carpeting and sprinting for the back exit to the soundtrack of his cackling laughter. The warm milk exploded against my hip, splashing me from shoulders to knees in sugary, sticky mess.

I ran hard across the grassy quad and toward the girls' locker room, not looking back.

"Attention students and staff," a voice boomed over the loudspeaker. I slid to a stop next to a soda machine and spun, but Cal hadn't chased me. "You are ordered by the county Sheriff's department to go directly home at this time and stay there." A pause. "A 6:00 p.m. curfew will be strictly enforced." Another pause. "God bless us all."

The emergency alarm screamed through the halls and pulsed from every classroom.

I hurried for the parking lot, joining the crowd of people headed the same way, and pulled my cell. "School's canceled," I texted my dad. "On my way home."

He didn't reply right away, but he kept his phone in his office, so if he was busy in the lab it might be a while.

The streets were congested and it took twice as long to get home. I steered my Honda with both hands fisted on the wheel. Twice, I narrowly avoided collisions with cars zigzagging through traffic.

My phone beeped. "Busy," Dad texted. "Move garage gear into panic room. See you tonight." I was too worried about dying on the road to stop and answer him.

The work trucks were gone from my driveway when I pulled up.

"Maya!" Mrs. Kinley came off her front porch with Freckles in a carrier. "Is your dad coming to get you?"

"He's in Raleigh," I said, "but he's been texting. He'll be home tonight."

"Okay." She popped the carrier into the backseat of her car. "I'm going to meet my parents in Nashville. You can come with me if you want. I'd love the company and 212R isn't as bad in the country as it is in the cities."

"I have to wait for my dad," I said. "He's really close to finding a cure."

She smiled wistfully. "Wouldn't that be wonderful."

"Be careful out there," I said and bolted myself inside my house.

I did what I'd been doing the last two weeks or so after school, as part of my dad's safety checklist. I stripped to my underwear in the laundry room and immediately took a hot shower in the hall bathroom. Only then did I change into comfy pants and a tank top and inspected our new panic room.

The crew had done a good job. It looked solid. Impenetrable, even. Our old pantry was now a metal cell with a heavy swinging door that sealed from the inside with a wheel crank. I crossed the square of extra soft carpeting and decided I could live there for a few days. As long as my dad was with me.

Speaking of, I texted him again. "Panic room is done. Looks sturdy."

While I waited for him to reply I made myself a sandwich and turned on the TV.

More bad news. Most of New York City was black and offline.

"The president has declared the entire city of New York a disaster zone," the reporter said. "The National Guard is on the ground as we speak doing all they can to quarantine plague sufferers and evacuate survivors." A video flashed on of a giant tank driving down a street choked with cars and people.

I didn't feel particularly optimistic about the military response. The threat to the city was a microscopic virus, not anything that could be shot or detained.

Done with my snack I followed my dad's directions. He'd been busy the last few weeks, even busier than I realized. Locked in our garage lay cases of drinking water and canned food, a first-aid kit, a tub of survival gear, and two narrow cots. I spent the afternoon sweeping up after the workers and moving and organizing the supplies into the old pantry.

"If you have a fever," the news anchor announced, "go immediately to the nearest emergency room."

I pressed the back of my hand to my forehead. So far so good.

"The best hope we have is to contain the virus," the reporter continued. "Once infected, though, you can spot a 'Red,' as some folks are calling them, by the red color of their eyes. We now have Dr. LaVay from the CDC to tell us more about why and how 212R affects the color of our irises. Doctor?"

I turned off the TV and texted Dad, "Lasagna for dinner? I'll start at 5."

While I waited to hear from him I collected

my guitar from my room and strummed a song I had written the year before called "Red Shoelaces."

When the tray of frozen vegetable lasagna was hot and ready at six I served myself and ate in front of the television. Every five minutes or so I checked my cell to see if my dad texted anything and I had missed the beep, but nothing came in.

"Many of the services we take for granted," the reporter said, "will no longer be available as early as tomorrow morning along the entire eastern seaboard. 212R has spread so quickly, incapacitating so many people, there may not be enough qualified people to run power, water, and sanitation services."

I set my dinner in the trash and double-checked that all the doors and windows were locked tight and then turned on my phone. No new messages.

"We here at the news desk will keep reporting," she added, "as long as we can to get you the information you need to stay safe. If the power in your area goes out, don't panic. Scrolling on the screen right now are the radio channels broadcasting emergency information in your area. So, if you have a battery powered radio in your survival kit get it out and test the batteries."

Something that sounded like a firecracker popped outside the front door. Then twice more.

Gunfire? I couldn't be around gunfire. It reminded me of Mason and my mom and the horrible, awful thing that happened two years ago.

I ran to the window, but the street was deserted.

My cell screen was blank. No new messages, no new texts, no missed calls.

"Dad," I whispered at my phone. "Where are you?"

The power blinked off, draping the house in quiet, purplish dusk.

"Lights went out," I texted Dad. "What do I do?"

Somebody outside screamed. The living room window shattered. Someone or something in the yard growled like a pissed off panther.

I snatched my guitar, my song diary, and my iPad.

The front door crashed open, and I ran for it, slamming the bunker's door closed with a resounding *clank*.

Chapter Two

Two weeks later

My last and final water bottle sat on the floor completely unrepentant about what it was forcing me to do. Because it was the last amount of drinking water inside the panic room I was leaving the confines of my metal safety pen and venturing out into the world to find more.

In the weeks since I'd locked myself inside, the power had stayed off and no one had texted or called or come to find me.

I carefully packed a bag with what I considered the necessities. Fig cookies. My iPad, which I would never leave behind. It had too many precious images and files on it. My song diary and a pen. Unfortunately, I had to leave my guitar behind. I didn't know how far I'd have to walk to find water and it would slow me down.

I steadied myself and turned the crank in extreme slow motion, my ears pricked for the faintest sound.

Silence.

Through a narrow crack I surveyed the kitchen. All I sensed was a sour stench. Hopefully from the trash.

No movement. No sound beyond my own breathing.

It had been just as quiet for the last fourteen days as I'd checked off nights in the back of my song diary. Fourteen days of silence, the only light coming from a battery-powered lantern. Fourteen days of nothing but sad songs on my guitar, jumping jacks to stave off atrophy, and canned food full of preservatives.

I swung the bunker's door wider and wider until I was certain no red-eyed infected person was going to leap at me. Though the front door stood open and a light breeze ruffled the living room curtains, the house was empty.

Wincing, I stepped around the kitchen trashcan crawling with maggots and peered into the front yard.

Two cars sat abandoned in the middle of our cul-de-sac and random pieces of trash littered the ground and built up along fences, but otherwise it was a ghost town on my street.

More importantly, my Honda was the only vehicle parked in our driveway. My dad hadn't answered my texts and he hadn't driven home.

My insides felt as wiggly and unsettled as the contents of the kitchen trashcan.

Where was he?

Before I left the house, though, I had to find a weapon. The problem was, neither my dad nor I were violent types. There were no guns in the house. Not even a baseball bat or a golf club.

Then I remembered. It wasn't exactly a medieval mace, but my dad was a die-hard *Lord of the Rings* nerd. Hanging in his home office among hundreds of pieces of merchandise and memorabilia was a fully functional replica of the sword Sting. It was the closest thing to an actual weapon we possessed, not counting steak knives and blunt objects. I took it down off the wall and tucked it into a belt loop.

There. Ready.

I poked my head out the front door. No sign of either infecteds or survivors, so I eased across the front lawn and headed down Cherry Blossom Court and out of our cul-de-sac.

Were there people locked inside these homes? Some had their doors smashed open like mine. A lot of windows were broken. The house on the corner had a minivan *inside* its living room.

I crossed into a part of the subdivision I hadn't spent much time in. The third house down, the one with the pink door and cherry trees in the yard, wasn't too intimidating. I marched across the driveway and swung open the door, but the knob slipped from my hand and banged into the wall.

I froze as the sound reverberated through

the house, and then something moved in the kitchen. Not one. Not two. *Three* red-eyed zombies stepped into the foyer.

I didn't wait to see if they would strike first, but spun and sprinted for the street. By the shuffling and grunting behind me, they followed me. And these weren't slow-moving zombies. They weren't zombies at all, technically, and they ran almost as fast as I did.

There was nowhere to hide. None of the houses had second floors to hide in, and the three predators on my tail weren't giving me enough time to barricade myself anywhere. My breath whistling in my ears, I searched for a place to hide.

The curtains in a house on my right parted and a pale face appeared. No red eyes. Another survivor. I swerved closer. But the woman shook her head sharply at me and closed the curtains tight.

I ran on, passing her house, and racing down Cherry Blossom Court toward home even as my lungs burned and my sneakers flapped a staccato rhythm on the asphalt. Thump, thump, thump, *thump*. An awesome beat tailor-made for a simple three-chord melody. No lyrics yet, though.

I forced myself to ignore the high intensity song taking shape in my mind because I wasn't home free.

Three Reds counted as a whole pack.

That's what they were. Not groups, not clubs, not teams. *Packs*. Like so many violent, soulless carnivores.

My house was straight ahead.

The muscles up and down my legs tensed like metal bands as I pushed myself into a full sprint and left the zombies in the dust. I couldn't let them see where I lived or catch me before I swung the panic room door shut.

But the pack behind me wasn't my only problem. The entire street had been overrun since I'd left home. A lot had changed while I'd been searching for provisions. Zombies loitered in my yard, my Honda had a writhing infected in the backseat, and a hunch-backed Red stood in my open front door.

Just like that, everything I had built and gathered and protected was lost.

That home was the last one my dad had ever lived in. Its address had been on all our letters and bills and catalogs. Inside it was the hall closet where I kept school photos of my twin brother Mason, my mother's diaries, and the clay handprint I'd made in first grade.

Poof. Gone.

Worst of all, my guitar was in there. It and the song diary in the pack on my back were all I had left in the world that brought me any kind of pleasure.

Bile in my throat, I veered right. My pack pinched my shoulders, and the hilt of my short sword dug into my right flank, but I didn't let either slow me down. I had to get to higher ground.

So I scrambled up the lattice on the side of Mrs. Kinley's house, digging my shoes into window framing and scraping my arms on the roof shingles so bad they bled.

On her roof I would be safe to take a few minutes to calm my racing heart and construct a plan. Because I really didn't want to leave my home. There was nowhere else to go.

A scream for help sounded behind me, and I flinched, my pulse exploding into overdrive. I craned my neck. Reds moaned sometimes, but I'd been secluded for so many days that the sound of someone else's terror captured my attention one hundred percent.

Where had they come from?

Was it possible they'd been living nearby and as well hidden as I'd been? Were there uninfected people holed up in their own mini fortresses all over town? All over the world? Because after six weeks of complete isolation I'd come to believe I was the last human on earth.

It was both exciting and alarming to realize I wasn't.

Behind me, in the path of the pack that had swollen to six Reds, a flush-faced woman dragged a young girl by the hand. The lady stumbled before righting herself. She was no runner. And neither was the little girl. She struggled to keep up.

I didn't call out.

I'd been alone a long time. Even before the infection my dad had worked long hours and, added with his daily commute, I'd spent a lot of time by myself listening to music and writing songs on my guitar. It was the main reason I'd avoided contamination.

Unless the two girls found a hiding spot pronto they would soon be overtaken by the pack. I rooted for them, even though I didn't reveal my position. Maybe my pale neighbor hiding behind her curtains had the right idea. Like a nervous tick, my fingers spelled out *h-i-d-e*, a holdover from a childhood spent signing with my deaf twin brother.

But the woman spotted me on my neighbor's roof anyway, even as quiet and low as I was, and she honed in on me as if I was the answer to her prayers.

My skin got all prickly and hot. I wasn't anyone's saving grace.

The exhausted woman turned on her inner boosters and made it to Mrs. Kinley's house seconds before the pack. Like some kind of superhero she grabbed the little girl by the waist and tossed her up at me.

Without thinking, I caught the child's hands. I pulled her onto the roof beside me, and then reached for the woman. She planted one foot on the wall and grabbed both my hands.

The pack, a tidal wave of writhing arms and teeth and elbows, slammed into her. She was yanked out of my grasp, and I nearly tumbled after her into the cluster of growling and grunting Reds but caught myself at the last second. This was the closest I'd ever been to zombies, and they were scarier and fiercer than I'd ever imagined.

"Get her out of here!" the woman shouted.

Then it got real quiet except for the wet sounds of feeding.

I scrambled away from the edge, and the little girl collapsed onto my lap in a gasping, sobbing heap. Her arms locked around my waist like a metal vice, squeezing until it hurt and leaving no room for escape. Little girls with messy blonde curls didn't normally frighten me, but my chest tightened and breathing became more difficult.

"Don't shake hands," my dad had said about a thousand times.

And there I was in a bear hug with a stranger.

It took a few seconds to assure myself I wasn't going to catch 212R from this little girl.

Tapping her arm, I whispered, "I can't breathe."

She sniffed and pulled away, but kept the entire right side of her body, from shoulder to thigh, plastered to mine. I hadn't been touched in so long it didn't feel reassuring. It felt uncomfortable. I tried to stand, but she allowed me no personal space. She embraced me around the middle again, tucking her blonde head into my belly.

"It's okay." I awkwardly patted her ear, not sure how to soothe her. I'd never had a little sister. My twin brother Mason had never needed comforting. He was too tough for hugs, even when we were little.

"Was she your mom?" A bad taste flooded my mouth. I knew all about losing a mother.

The girl thumped her head against my midsection in a back and forth motion. "Willa took care of me."

"Was it just the two of you?" If she came from a group, I could deliver her back to them and be gone.

"Yes."

Great. Which meant it was now just the two of us. Because no matter how much safer it was on my own, I couldn't abandon a child to the Reds. Not that she'd let me, anyway. Her arms remained looped above my hips.

I wracked my brain for a new game plan.

My house was overrun with zombies, now exiting the front door to investigate the pack feeding beneath us. If there hadn't been so many, I might have tried to take back my house, but I'd never make it inside. Even as fast as I was.

Who knew how many Reds hid, unseen,

inside my home.

I had to leave it all behind. Everything I owned and loved. Stockpiles of food and toiletries. Clothes. My bed. Photos. My guitar. All I had left was the pack on my back and my dad's replica sword on my hip. A pang of grief, fresh and raw, pinged through my chest.

The little girl sniffled. "Is she dead?"

I didn't have to look to answer definitively. "Yes. What's your name?"

"Hunny Green." She wiped at her face without letting go of me, streaking her cheeks with dirt. "What's yours?"

"Maya Solomon. Can you run?"

"I'm tired."

Though my pulse was back within normal range, I was still breathing heavily. Sweat tickled the sides of my face and the small of my back. The air was so thick with moisture it had substance, and I would be in big trouble if I didn't replenish the fluids leaking from my pores and saturating my clothes.

I wet my lips, finding them dry and peeling. If I didn't locate fresh water soon I was never going to make it to Raleigh.

I turned my back on my house because my stomach ached at the sight of zombies coming out of the front door. But the area around us wasn't much more promising. Especially when the two packs below us merged and laid siege to our hiding place.

"Catch your breath. We're leaving." I patted her back again in a slower beat. Like the rhythm of an R&B song. Patta-pat-pat-patta-pat-pat.

She stared up at me with big, shiny green eyes. "Where are you taking me?"

"Another house," I said, making it up as I went along. Because I didn't know what else to do.

"How old are you?" I asked.

She squeezed me in short, painful pulses. "Eight."

I hoped she was a mature eight because getting out of the neighborhood was going to be tricky.

The cul-de-sac to the south was crawling with Reds, but open land spread out behind my walled neighborhood to the west. No houses, no streets, just a field of grass and pine forests in the distance. Beyond the trees poked the tops of buildings in the next town over. And standing in the middle of that open stretch of dry, grassy waste was a lone zombie.

Just one.

All by himself.

Watching me.

Zombies didn't travel alone. They hunted in packs. Maybe this one was wounded.

I hated the idea of running straight at a Red, but one was easier to outsmart than twenty. It was the best option I had.

I dragged Hunny to the far side of the

sloping roof, our feet getting all tangled up because she refused to let go of my sweat drenched shirt. Below us stood a plastic playhouse atop a wedge of dead grass, and then a cinder block wall. If I could get the little girl over that wall, we were free.

Once we were out of sight of the two packs, now converging in Mrs. Kinley's driveway, I could take time to devise a plan. A better one. Like finding another safe house. A two-story model. I could cover the ground floor with plywood or building scraps and live in relative safety on the second floor.

Then, in the back of my mind another option took shape.

A cure exists.

Two weeks earlier my dad's antiserum had been close to the human testing and mass production stages. If I found it and got it to the right people, a new world could slowly take shape atop the old one.

It would be dangerous to make the journey into Raleigh alone and on foot. Food, water, and shelter would be scarce. Packs of vicious Reds clearly outnumbered us.

But if I was the only person alive who had knowledge about the cure, could I let it rot in my dad's lab? And what would my dad want me to do?

He'd paid a lot of money to install the panic room in our house to protect me from all the dangers in the world. By traveling to his lab I would be anything but safe.

I glanced at Hunny, my curly haired tagalong. What did she, and other survivors like her, want me to do? Find the cure or forget it?

"I'll lower you," I said, "and when I get down I'll help you over the wall."

"I'm scared."

"This is nothing." I kept a hold of one of her arms and, without giving her a chance to chicken out, I pushed her off the ledge.

Hunny screamed and kicked and tried to tear my hand off, but she toppled gently onto the playhouse roof, and then rolled onto the grass. I followed, got her over the wall, scrambled after, and we were safe.

One Red stood between us and freedom.

"Run as fast as you can," I told Hunny. "He'll chase us, but we can lose him in the trees." I snatched her hand and sprinted for the pine forest, pulling her behind me.

"Shoot him," she panted, dragging on my arm.

I didn't have a gun. Only a short, engraved sword. And I didn't intend to get close enough to the zombie to use it.

"Just keep running."

We passed near enough to the Red to see the ruby color of his eyes and the name *Ben* stitched above the pocket of a navy blue work shirt. He had dark hair, even darker than mine, and was filthy from head to toe. He pivoted as we passed within five yards of him.

We made brief eye contact, and his mouth parted as if he recognized me. But that was impossible. People lost higher brain function after infection. Things like compassion, critical thinking, and memory were switched off. Maybe lost forever.

I'd been afraid to venture out for supplies in case I bumped into a zombie I'd known before the red plague hit. A teacher or a neighbor or even a friend.

But I got a good look at this one. I didn't know him.

As we neared Ben, I silently pleaded with him to cooperate and let us pass unharmed. But he only hesitated about half a minute before giving chase. His heavy work boots pounded upon the grass behind us, a bass drum in a rock anthem.

This was a big mistake. I knew better than to approach a Red, even one by itself.

Hunny and I ran straight for a thick-trunked tree with low branches.

I shoved the little girl onto a sturdy branch about six feet off the ground and then swung up beside her like a gymnast. My backpack and sword made me awkward, but I crawled to my feet seconds before Ben skidded to a halt under our tree.

Squealing, Hunny climbed to the next

highest branch, putting herself well out of reach of the lone Red. I pulled up on the same branch, but it was weaker than the one under my feet, and the wood creaked.

My heart racing, I let go of Hunny's perch and gripped the rough trunk even if my feet weren't high enough off the ground to be safe. Ben was tall and my sneakers were only slightly above his eye level.

Ben shuffled from foot to foot, growling.

I had nowhere to hide or anyway to climb higher. Fifteen feet separated me from the nearest tree. There wasn't another branch on our pine strong enough to hold me.

Wiping sweat from my eyes with my shoulder, I resolved to hang on to the tree until I couldn't hang on anymore.

"Maya!" Hunny reached for me. "Hurry. Climb up."

"It's okay," I said, keeping an eye on the Red.

After infection, bathing wasn't a priority. Neither were balanced nutrition or personal hygiene. He was grimy and emaciated. Dark fluid stained his clothes and skin. His hands were so dirty he may as well have soaked them in ink. And his blood red eyes seemed to glow as he stared at me. *Through* me.

Hunny whined like a lost puppy. "Hold my hand? I'm scared, Maya."

Not willing to take my eyes off Ben, I

reached up blindly, and her small fingers gripped mine.

The Red lifted his arms, and I hugged the rough trunk even tighter. If he yanked on my ankles I had to be strong enough to resist.

"Stab him," Hunny shrieked. "Kill him!"

Even if I wanted to take another person's life, I didn't dare let go of the tree to pull my short sword and put myself off balance.

The Red set his hands on the branch beside my feet. I held my breath, my whole body quivering like a fresh guitar string as I waited for him to grab me.

"Don't let go of the tree," I whispered to myself. "Don't let go…"

Ben didn't appear hungry. Or filled with killer rage. He stared back at me, a curious expression on his dirty face as if he found me utterly fascinating.

He withdrew his hands and backed up half a dozen feet.

The breath whooshed out of me, and I went limp against the trunk of the tree. The flesh-hungry zombie hadn't dragged me to the ground and tore out my insides. He'd let me go.

On news reports in the days leading up to my locking myself into a bunker I'd witnessed Reds run at full speed. I'd seen them attack with an inhuman ferocity. I'd watched, fascinated, as one tore a garden shed to splinters to get at a dog cowering inside. But I'd never seen or heard of a Red turning away from easy prey.

Ben paced, a low, guttural growl emanating from between clenched jaws. "Mmrrr. Mmmrrr."

"I think we'll be okay," I said to Hunny. "We'll stay here until dawn. Let go of my hand." Traveling at night was too dangerous. I couldn't see well enough to avoid meandering zombies, and without a good hiding place I'd be cooked. Even if I sprinted I could run straight into another pack.

My watch read six thirty. Dinner time. My stomach rumbled right on cue.

"Then go where?"

Good question.

I'd leave Hunny with the first people we found, and then I'd acquire a house with an upstairs. I could live there indefinitely, safe and secure. When it was quiet, I'd go on supply runs until I built up a decent stockpile. It was more or less the life I'd been leading for the past two weeks. I knew exactly how to survive that way.

But there was another option. Out there, no more than a day's walk away, lay my dad's lab. He'd spent his final days and hours creating a cure. If I found the elixir and somehow delivered it to an educated survivor for analysis and eventual distribution to plague victims, then this nightmare would be over.

My dad would want his work to mean something. He hadn't given up on a cure. Even when he should have stayed home and away from contagion, he'd gone to work to help save us all.

I would finish what he started.

"Tomorrow we're going to Raleigh," I announced, glancing down at Ben. "We're going to wipe out the red plague."

A cure exists.

Chapter Three

Sleep had been agonizingly out of reach all night. I didn't trust Ben enough to sit on the branch and close my eyes. So I spent the night standing, hugging the coarse bark of the tree, and holding hands with Hunny until my shoulder muscles gave up.

Several times I'd suffered waking nightmares that the sun would never come up and I'd be trapped forever in a tree with a little girl above me and a hungry Red below. Fortunately, the earth kept turning and as the sun rose and cast warm light onto my face, I slipped out of my pack and inventoried my meager provisions.

During the night my sweat-soaked clothes had dried out, but now my mouth was chalky.

I still had fig cookies, but no water. My first priority, after escaping Ben, had to be fresh water or it wouldn't matter what else happened.

"I'm thirsty," Hunny murmured.

Me too. "I don't have anything to drink."

"What!"

"I got chased by Reds before I found any."

She huffed a disappointed sigh. "This sucks."

I sorted the rest of my possessions, but one thing wasn't where it should have been. My clicker pen, the Hello Kitty one I wrote songs with, had been snug in the side pocket of my pack yesterday. But it was missing. No sign of it in the grass and pine needles beneath me. Like everything else I'd ever cared about, it was gone.

At the very bottom of my backpack I carried what was most important to me, the things I would never be parted from. My iPad with the final pictures of my family in it. My song diary. But besides the cookies there was nothing to cook with, no first-aid, and no matches or tools.

I replaced my pack and drew my short sword.

Far to my right a tapping sound started up, ran through a nice and even staccato rhythm, and then ceased. A woodpecker, probably. Or the wind blowing a gate against a wall. It was amazing the noises I heard after all the human sounds went away.

Hunny stirred above me. "That was the worst night of my life."

It wasn't the worst night of my life. There was the first night after my mom was killed, and the night after Mason was arrested. And the night my dad didn't come home from work.

There had been some rough nights in the bunker when I'd wondered if I was the last uninfected survivor alive in the whole world. In the dark the loss of so many billions of people had hit me the hardest. I'd had more nightmares tucked inside the panic room than I'd ever had as a child in my bed.

Tonight wasn't even in my top ten.

"Mr. Zombie's still there, Maya." Hunny's voice squeaked. "Why don't you kill him already?"

"We don't have to kill every Red we meet," I said, eyeing Ben. He was about my age, seventeen, or maybe a little older. He stared right back. "We can outrun him."

He hadn't slept once, but he'd paced, and then circled the tree, and then stood like a statue. No matter where he'd moved he'd always kept me in his sights.

Nothing about him made sense. Ben didn't run with a pack. He wasn't obsessed with tearing the bloody organs from living bodies and consuming them raw. But he was unusually interested in Hunny and me. I'd never heard of a Red acting so *human*. If I hadn't seen his crimson-colored eyes up close, I would have wondered if he was infected at all.

"Here's the plan," I stated, craning my neck to see into Hunny's face. "I'll jump down, and then you'll jump down. We're going to run our butts off in that direction." I pointed northwest toward Raleigh. Woods and then the suburbs stood in our way. "No matter what happens, keep running. Can you do that?"

"Where are you taking me?"

"To my dad's lab in Raleigh. I told you already."

I gestured for Hunny to stay still on her upper branch until I could evaluate Ben's attitude this morning and whether we could get out of this tree without being attacked.

Contrary to the color of his irises, he made no aggressive advances. No more guttural noises. But his blood red eyes tracked my every move.

"Hunny?" I began in my calmest voice, the kind you used around strange dogs. "I'm going now. If Ben attacks right away, just stay in the tree."

"I'm scared." She whined once, and then was quiet.

The odds of making it safely away from the Red were good. Since he hadn't attacked us yet. Maybe he had brain damage or some other invisible injury. All I had to do was run fast. And I was a very fast runner.

My fingers fluttered, signing the letters r-u-n several times. A nervous twitch.

I tightened the straps on my pack, adjusted my sword, and stepped away from the tree trunk. The branch under my sneakers squeaked. Silently, Ben shifted from one foot to the other. I crouched down, got a good hold on the branch, and swung off. I hit my feet and froze for a split second.

Ben growled. "Mmmmrr." But he didn't come any closer.

"Hurry, Hunny," I said, reaching up. "Jump. I'll catch you."

She didn't hesitate. But I'd underestimated the weight of an eight-year-old, even a half-starving one. Fifty pounds of terrified little girl hit me high in the chest and we both crashed into the hard, sandy ground.

I was on my feet in a blink, leading Hunny deeper into the trees. I didn't wait to see if Ben chased us. I just ran. It didn't matter how tired I was or sore or thirsty. I ran as fast as Hunny let me, heading north, away from my home, and toward my dad's lab.

"I can't go any faster," she shouted.

"Yes, you can!"

I dragged Hunny through scrub brush and kudzu and around trees as tall as skyscrapers, stiff and craggy branches tearing at our clothes and faces, for what must have been a mile.

And then I really messed up. I got distracted by Hunny's crying, gasping pleas and didn't see the exposed root until it was too late. My boot caught, I did a sort of pirouette in midair, and slammed into the ground. Knifing pain tore through my right knee.

I tried to stand, but the moment I put weight

on my leg it crumpled, and I tasted dirt again.

It was one thing to walk away from my house. It wasn't gone, just invaded. I could always return in a few days, clear it out, and reinforce. I'd left my guitar behind, but I could find another one. Maybe even a better one. But without my speed, how was I going to survive? If I couldn't run from Reds I'd have to fight them. And I was no good at fighting.

I forced oxygen in and out with even, measured breaths. Because I wasn't going to give up and cry in the dirt. Not yet.

"You," Hunny panted, "okay?"

Before risking an answer, I scanned the trees for a lone Red in a navy blue work shirt, but I saw only low hanging branches and pinecones.

"I twisted my knee." The longer I remained on my feet the better I felt. "I'll be okay. Just no more running."

Maybe, as with a sprained ankle, a little rest and some willpower and I'd be better in a few minutes. I hobbled forward, but the moment I put the tiniest bit of weight on my right leg the pain popped. Gritting my teeth, I hopped forward using the evergreens for leverage.

Sweat dribbled along my hairline and a wave of dizziness hit me hard. Running in the late spring heat and humidity was draining the last of my reserves. I craved water, but there was none to guzzle down.

"How are you going to take care of me?"

Hunny asked. "You're too hurt to do anything."

Take care of her? I hadn't asked for her companionship. In fact, she'd been thrust at me without my consent. I would have been better off alone. I knew how to survive on my own, but I hadn't the first idea how to take care of a little kid.

My brother Mason had been like her — selfish. Demanding. I'd hated it when he'd bossed me around, and it was even worse when Hunny did it.

I almost yelled at her to leave, but I wouldn't abandon her in the middle of a North Carolina pine forest. Sure, I wanted to get rid of her, but not like that. So I swallowed my frustration and shuffled forward.

"I'm fine." I hopped to the next tree, making a lot of noise. Not on purpose, but on one leg it was difficult to be quiet. The contents of my pack jostled. Dry needles, pinecones, and twigs crackled.

Reds were attracted by noise.

"I'm sorry. I didn't mean it." Hunny wedged herself under my right armpit. She was a scrawny kid, but she had strong shoulders. Leaning on her helped me hop faster.

"I'm hungry," she said. "Do you have granola bars?"

I wished. "I have fig cookies."

"Ew!" She gagged. "I'd rather eat barf."

"It doesn't matter. We can't stop anyway."

Ben was close behind. There was no cover anywhere in sight. And I couldn't climb a tree in my present condition. I had to keep walking until I found a building. Even a barn or a shed would've done at that point.

"I haven't eaten in two days." She fluttered her beautiful green eyes and stuck out her lower lip.

Rolling my eyes, I asked, "You didn't eat yesterday, either?"

She shook her head and blonde curls, about a week from being full dreadlocks, bounced. If I didn't brush her hair soon it would be unbrushable.

"We ran out, and Willa couldn't find any more."

It didn't seem possible, but I hadn't eaten since breakfast the day before. And that had been pretzels and my last bottle of water. I paused just long enough to pull the package of fig cookies out of my pack and offer them to Hunny.

"Yuck." She squished up her freckled nose. "I hate those."

"Suit yourself." The scent of sweet dough and fruit had my stomach growling, and I shoved two in my mouth. "You can eat when we get to Raleigh." The treat ground to paste in my dry mouth, refusing to go down my throat. Throwing my head back, I forced the food down. "There might be safe places to look there." Or maybe not.

Though I didn't know how we'd make it downtown in our present condition. Forty-five minutes away by car, if there was no gridlock. But on foot? *Walking*?

Not only did I not have a home to hide in, but I had a scrawny eight-year-old clinging to me like a monkey, the weather was doing its best to kill me, and I couldn't even walk properly, let alone run from the Reds sure to sniff us out. The idea of ever finding my dad's lab seemed like a pipe dream.

"Fine," Hunny huffed, stealing a handful of soft cookies from my bag. "I'll have some."

Maybe with a working vehicle we could drive into the city. But that would take even more time and cause a lot of unnecessary noise. With no real weapons and no safe place to hide I preferred to keep walking.

"Can't we sit down for a while?" Hunny asked, finishing the final fig cookie.

How had she survived this long with such awful instincts? "If we take a break," I explained, "that Red from last night, Ben, will find us. We can't stop until we get to a safe place."

A branch snapped behind us. I didn't see anyone in the trees, but either way, it was time to go. I grabbed Hunny and used her strength to help propel us both north toward the city.

Chapter Four

We stepped out of the cooler shade of a pine forest onto an exposed access lane behind a large subdivision of nearly identical, pastel-hued homes. This community hadn't fared as well as mine. White smoke curled away from the charred remains of a two-story home. A pair of feral dogs fought over a human body lying in the gutter. Someone had painted "HELP ME" across his or her garage door.

I paused, taking the weight off my right knee. These people had experienced a level of fear and desperation that still lingered in the air. I may have been alone and uneasy on my cul-de-sac, but I'd never been afraid for my life. My sanity, yeah, but not my life. Setting up camp in one of these run-down houses was the last thing I wanted to do.

Uncomfortable with so many signs of anguish, I turned my back on the whole neighborhood. In the distance, peeking above swaths of green pines, were the tops of high-rises. My dad's lab was somewhere out there, nestled among all those buildings, waiting for me to find it.

"We're not going through the subdivisions," I warned Hunny, who was already inspecting a fallen two-wheeler in someone's driveway. If she sensed the sorrow in the atmosphere she didn't let on. "We're going to try to walk all the way to Raleigh today." Though in this heat, with my aching knee, and no water we probably wouldn't make it until tomorrow.

"Here, ride this," Hunny offered. "Pretend it's a wheelchair."

I opened my mouth to politely decline, but on second thought, it wasn't a bad idea. I'd move faster on two wheels than I could hopping around on one leg.

"We're still not going through the neighborhoods," I said, finding the right balance on the bike because my sword and backpack kept tilting me. I hadn't ridden a bicycle since I was a little kid. "Stay close."

"I'll look for a real wheelchair."

"I'll be okay."

And I would be. On the track team I'd had plenty of sprained ankles, twisted knees, and sore feet. This too would heal. Nothing was broken, just torn. An ice pack would help, not that I was going to find one of those.

After ten minutes of the most awkward bicycle outing ever, I wasn't sure which was worse, scooting along on two wheels or hopping on one leg. Every time I pushed off with my left foot the chain rattled and I coasted a few feet. *Push*, coast. *Push*, coast.

But I wasn't sweating anymore, and that was a big plus.

"Why are you all by yourself?" Hunny blurted out.

I'd been on my own for what felt like forever. Two weeks since Dad hadn't come home, but even before the plague he'd worked long hours and I'd kept myself entertained after school. I'd often prepared my own dinners and gone to bed before he even drove into the garage.

But that's not what the girl meant. "My family's gone. I'm the only one who survived." Though I didn't know if the red virus had taken my dad and brother, it all amounted to the same thing. Gone was gone.

Because if Dad or Mason had avoided 212R, and then the zombies, they would have found me by now. For days I'd held out a strong, unshakable hope that Mason would escape juvenile detention and then Dad would find a safe route through the city and they'd both come home to Cherry Blossom Court. As if nothing bad had ever happened, my brother and my dad would walk up our driveway and knock on the bunker door.

But after two weeks, I'd given up on that

dream.

"Yeah," Hunny sighed. "I guess my family's all gone, too."

She jogged over and gave me a shove. I coasted even further. Giggling, she ran beside me, pushing me down a hill.

"Thanks, but keep the noise down," I warned. Reds were attracted by sound, and we'd already produced more than our share.

I cruised past a Ford truck with all its windows shattered. And then I saw it. The I–40. And I knew we would be okay, after all.

The massive, six-lane highway beginning west in Barstow, California and ending in nearby Wilmington, North Carolina was a two-thousand-mile-long ribbon of commuter technology, a grand symbol of everything the human race could accomplish and everything we'd lost. And it led straight into the heart of Raleigh.

A month ago it had been a busy super highway, but it had become an automobile graveyard. It was a packed parking lot of abandoned vehicles in various stages of ruin. Some were crumpled from accidents. Some had their doors pried open by vandals. Some looked shiny and untouched. But none of them were moving any time soon.

I ditched the bike at the on-ramp when space became limited and tapped a comforting beat on the trunk of a Prius with my fingernail.

Ticky-tick. Ticky-tock.

Since the red virus hit I hadn't been able to write a decent song. Before people got sick I'd been writing love songs and catchy country tunes every day. And then, like turning off a light, Dad hadn't come home and I couldn't string words to a melody to save my life.

But something about the mess of empty vehicles and the fresh air and the simple rhythm triggered my muse. *Way down here. I disappear.*

No, that was too miserable a thought. I didn't want to compose a sad song. But I'd keep working on it. I repeated the rhythm a few more times to get it good and stuck in my head because I couldn't record it on my iPad, and I'd left my guitar behind. All I had were my memories and the diary in my pack. I shifted the backpack around, knocking the short sword hanging from my belt.

Everything was so different…

"I thought you said zombies are attracted by noise," Hunny shouted. "Why are you tapping on the car?"

Ignoring her, I said, "We'll follow the highway into Raleigh. And if you see water bottles, *please* say something."

"I'll look for zombies, too." Showing off, Hunny sprang onto the hood of a white Nissan and leap-frogged three cars ahead, scrambling over roofs and sliding down windshields.

I followed more slowly, picking

unobstructed paths through the jumble of cars and trucks and using the vehicles as crutches.

In my junior year I'd trained as a sprinter. My track coach timed me at just over five minutes per mile. A six-minute mile was easier. If I ran at half speed along the guardrail, Raleigh was about three hours away. But my knee wasn't getting better. In fact, the flesh around my joint was swollen tight and hot to the touch. Running was out of the question. I couldn't even walk on my own. We were clocking a thirty-minute mile at best, which meant it would be hours, maybe the whole day, before we got to Raleigh.

I pushed off the doorframe of a luxury sedan with a discarded laptop on the front seat. There were no bodies in any of these cars, thank goodness. The infection, back when it was passed in handshakes, kisses, sneezes, and coughs, took three days to incubate inside a person. Three days to realize their fever was too high and wouldn't go down, no matter what medicine they took. Three days to realize they were going to be a flesh-eating zombie.

People trying to flee the cities had clogged up freeways like this one. Hopelessly stuck, they must have walked, en masse, down the road before the three days were up and they lost all higher-level thinking.

I'd seen aerial footage of highways turned to parking lots and people streaming through them, children and luggage on their backs.

After watching coverage like that, I'd often fantasized how I would have spent my final three days of normal life. It didn't matter anymore. There was hardly anything fun left, anyway. No more concerts. No roller coasters. No five-star resorts. But if given the chance, I would've traveled somewhere during my last feverish days.

I would have flown to Paris. Or London. Or Moscow. I would have stuffed my face with all the cheeseburgers and chocolate brownie ice cream I could stomach. And then, my guitar strapped to my back, I would've found a warm spot on a quiet beach and waited for full infection to destroy everything about me.

Hunny jumped off a sports car and ducked behind a pickup truck.

"What did you find?" I called.

"Nothing." She reappeared with a blank look and empty hands.

The girl made me nervous. I didn't know a thing about her. Where she'd come from. How she'd avoided infection.

"How did you find Willa?" I asked.

"My mommy and daddy sent me to a hospital," Hunny said softly. "They were so nice. They bought me a lot of things." She looked up at me. "I had every one of the Saddle Club Girls. Do you know what those are? They're dolls." She mimicked rocking a baby in her bony arms.

"You dress them up and fix their hair, and they all had their own pony and—"

"Hunny," I said. "What about Willa?"

"Oh." She shrugged. "Mommy and Daddy made me go to a special hospital so I wouldn't get sick. But everyone there got sick too except Willa and me. We ran away."

So Hunny's parents had been wealthy enough to send her to a quarantined hospital. For a lot of money, staff kept their clients healthy and virus free. But not even bleach, sterile gloves, and a high-tech security system had a chance against 212R. News channels had loved to run stories of hospitals overrun with disease. No one place was safer than any other.

"How did you get into my neighborhood yesterday?" I asked. We weren't near any hospitals or quarantines.

"After our house got attacked we started looking for another house, but there were zombies."

Speaking of…

I checked over my right shoulder and then my left. No Reds. Except for a few chattering birds searching for food scraps we were alone on the highway. Ben must have lost interest in us and went off in search of an easier meal. I wouldn't have minded him following us, as strange as it sounded, just to see what he'd do next. But he wasn't anywhere in sight, and that was probably for the best.

I had enough problems without a zombie on my tail.

I took another breather against a four-wheel-drive truck, flexing my right knee and then my ankle. It only marginally helped the pain.

Without warning the birds went quiet in mid trill, and then scattered into the skies.

My pulse spiked. I needed a place to hide.

I didn't want to hurt anyone, not even the Reds, but they had no conscience or human compassion. I had to protect not only my own neck, but also the little girl's.

Except I didn't know the first thing about mortal combat. Yeah, I'd been in karate when I was seven but the skills hadn't stuck. Over Christmas I'd volunteered at a local hospital, but knowing how to take a blood pressure wouldn't help me now. My dad had taught me to be clean, not to fight.

Four zombies, three males and a female, trudged around a bend in the highway headed in our direction.

I ditched my backpack, snapped my fingers to get Hunny's attention, and dropped to the trash-strewn asphalt, hot to the touch. It was no use trying to climb on top of a car or barricading us inside one. The moment the Reds saw us they would attack. They couldn't climb but they would wait us out, tearing the vehicle to pieces of twisted metal until they pulled us out like plucking tuna from a tin can.

Hunny was a child, but she knew when to shut up. Thank goodness.

I slid over rough road, scraping the already scratched skin of my palms and forearms, and wrenching my knee so hard I teared up. Hunny scuttled beside me like a crab.

I tensed, my breath a locomotive in my head. People in Denver heard me panting.

Slow, uneven footsteps grew louder. Hunny made a hand sign for *gun* in front of my face. I shook my head. Maybe the little girl didn't know how a single bullet could rip a person's life to pieces so badly it could never be put back together. But I did.

My brother Mason had pulled a trigger and taken our mother away forever.

I would never carry one, let alone use one.

The Reds shambled closer, and my breathing grew even more out of control as I pictured their faces in my mind—blank red eyes, slack mouths, dirt and blood and who knew what else on their chins and cheeks and hands.

Two pairs of bare feet, one pair of brown boots, and one pair of leather sandals stepped into the path between a white delivery van and us. They sniffed and snorted and shuffled within three feet of our hiding spot.

The group paused and I knew, just *knew*, we were about to be dragged out kicking and screaming and then beaten to death. As a last resort I found finger holds in the smelly engine above me in order to hang on as long as possible.

Hunny gripped my shirt, and I was afraid even that whisper of sound would attract them. I held my breath.

New footsteps approached in double time. Someone else had found us. *Five* Reds versus one little girl and me?

Fists hit flesh and several of the Reds let loose frustrated groans.

No way… I knew Reds killed each other. They had to in order to find enough blood and flesh to eat. But I'd never watched a zombie brawl on the news.

One by one, the four zombies that had sniffed us out fell beside our hiding spot until a single pair of black work boots stood inches from my face. A strangely familiar pair of boots.

At home, my family had signed everything we said for Mason. My brother and I had signed together our whole lives. It was an instinct to spell out *B-e-n* with my right hand for Hunny to read.

But she didn't know what I was doing and looked at me with a stunned expression. She waved her hand wildly between us, mocking me. I made a mental note to teach her the alphabet later. If we were going to be together for a while we should be able to converse silently and across distances.

Suddenly Ben's face appeared in the space between car and asphalt. He reached for me and his fingers left three bloody bands across my forearm.

Swallowing a startled squeak, I shoved Hunny hard in the opposite direction. "Get out. Go. Run." Following awkwardly, I hopped to my feet and bounced after her one-legged. She was faster than me, but I stayed with her for at least half a mile before I stopped to look back.

Ben wasn't chasing us. He hadn't moved an inch. We made brief eye contact, and then he bent over what must have been the bodies of the four Reds he'd attacked.

To protect us.

But Reds didn't protect survivors. In fact, their strongest instinct was to feed. They didn't have any other desire. More likely, he'd chased us all morning through the trees and the abandoned subdivision, killing the other four Reds in order to eat before he turned on us. That made more sense.

I stared at the bloody marks he'd left on my arm. Three wet bands.

It was possible Ben's behavior wasn't that unusual. Maybe the infected were evolving or even getting better.

"Maya, come on!" Hunny called from a hundred feet ahead.

I flinched at the sound of her voice, whipping around to check the surroundings. No new Reds. It was just me and Hunny and Ben. The birds had returned, though, and they chirped merrily as they foraged for crumbs.

We had to keep moving.

Ben's protecting us, or at least seeming to protect us, couldn't distract me from getting to Raleigh.

Something rustled behind us, something big. I spun, expecting to see another zombie, ready to either hide or fight. But it wasn't a Red standing between two compact cars growling at me, it was a starving black Labrador with its head lowered and its eyes trained on Hunny.

As a kid I'd pleaded with my parents for a dog. I thought they were the most huggable, lovable, most adorable creatures in the world. I begged. I wrote letters to Santa. I called Grandma in West Virginia. My favorite breed was the Boston terrier and as a little kid, about Hunny's age, I'd spent hours drawing pictures of black and white, snub-nosed puppies I would name Princess or Queenie or Sparkle.

But my mom was allergic to dogs. And not slightly sensitive to dander. No, she was full-blown break into hives and suffer a sinus infection allergic. A dog would never be in our future. By the time the truth settled into my consciousness I'd wasted a lot of time and emotional energy wanting something I could never have.

"Here, buddy," I cooed, offering my hand to sniff. He looked soft, and I desperately wanted to pet him. I constructed an entire fantasy in my head in those brief few seconds where the dog became my loyal and affectionate companion who would follow me everywhere, hunt for squirrels, and share them with me.

I'd call him Rooster and we would tackle this post-apocalyptic world as a team.

Were animals infected by the red plague? I'd often wondered things like that while alone in my panic room. Did their eyes go red too? Did they suddenly crave flesh and blood? Or was it only a human disease? Were there zombie hawks out there? Zombie hamsters? Zombie cockroaches, ants, and bees? Was every step beyond my four walls a minefield of infection and danger? It's one of the reasons I'd stayed in my home for so long, not knowing what the outside world was like after the red plague.

Rooster's head lowered even further and his upper lips curled back, revealing finger-sized canines. He growled like a chainsaw.

Two other dogs I hadn't seen walked out from behind one of the compact cars and created a chorus of snarling and snapping noises.

Their vocal aggression triggered something primal in me.

Hunny recognized the trouble we were in and screamed like a banshee, sticking to me with superglue.

"I can't run," I panted, my heart pounding in a weird, uneven rhythm. "I can't run."

The black lab launched itself at us, his

muscular legs pumping, his ribs showing in sharp relief through his dirty coat.

I stumbled a few steps, pushing off the cars around me, but it was obvious I couldn't outrun Rooster. He'd be on me in seconds and I had no defense against his nasty bite.

But I had lots of things to throw. I bent and gathered an empty tin can, a paperback, and a half eaten hard candy in the shape of a baby bottle, all litter that had blown against the tire of the car nearest me. I stood my ground, Hunny cowering behind me, and threw the tin can. It flew wide, but the dog took notice and slowed. I missed with the paperback, too.

The hard candy, though, hit Rooster directly on the snout. He halted about fifteen feet away, suddenly uncertain about his plan of attack. His dog friends followed his lead and pushed pause on the assault, stepping nervously from side to side and sniffing the air.

"Go chase a squirrel," I shouted at them. "We're not your dinner!" I pulled my short sword and waved it in the air. It worked. Some inbred fear of human beings reared to the surface in the black lab. He backed off, his tail down.

"Reverse it," I hissed at Hunny. "We're getting out of here fast."

"Are they going to bite me?"

I sent the dogs a good, long, hopefully intimidating look. They were still edging away, but I didn't trust their innate fear to outweigh their hunger forever. "No. But move it, just in case."

I grabbed the back of her shirt and we half ran, half hopped toward the next freeway off-ramp.

Eventually Hunny grew bored of outpacing me and lent me her shoulder again. I still wasn't accepting sidekick applications, but it wasn't completely horrible traveling with her. I was still dumping her skinny rear end first survivor I found, but she was okay. Spoiled, but sort of sweet.

"Hey," I said. "Let me teach you finger spelling. It's fun, and we can sign words to each other when we have to be quiet."

Hunny pulled a face. "What is it?"

"Sign language."

She perked up. "Oh. Okay."

"This is 'yes.' This is 'no.'" I showed her the simple signs. "A. B. C. Now, you." She copied the signs with minimal errors. I taught her the rest of the alphabet a few letters at a time, then made her repeat it.

On the eleventh pass she cried, "My hand hurts!" And quit.

I snapped my fingers to get her attention, and then spelled, "*T-o-o b-a-d.*"

She scrunched up her nose. "Tuba? What is that supposed to mean?"

"We'll keep practicing." I chuckled. "Start at

the beginning." I softly sang "The ABC Song," expecting her to follow along with her signs. Which she did after releasing a giant sigh.

I had a mental flashback to when Mason and I were just goofy little kids. It was a good feeling. Still smiling, I realized there were lots of things I could teach her. When I was eight I learned the multiplication tables and North Carolina history. Maybe I could show Hunny a few other things before I found her a new guardian.

"Whoa," Hunny said, stopping dead in her tracks.

Up ahead at the next off-ramp stood a shiny red and yellow McDonald's restaurant. Even after everything that had happened it still excited the little girl.

"Can we go there? Please?" She clasped her hands under her chin and stuck out her lower lip. "*Please?*"

"You know we can't make chicken nuggets and fries, right?" The best we could hope for inside the restaurant were canned and bagged ingredients that hadn't gone bad.

"I know." She hopped from one foot to the other. "I still want to go. It'll be fun."

"Fun." I snorted. I hadn't done anything *fun* in a long time. "Make it fast."

Chapter Five

I trudged across the trash-strewn parking lot sticking to the cooler shadows when possible, my gaze bouncing over anything and everything. There were no bird noises here, which gave me a twisting sensation in my gut. I listened for the faintest sounds of movement around the restaurant.

Nothing but garbage blowing under abandoned vehicles.

It was hard to imagine the mass exodus that had happened here and all over the country. Where had so many people gone? Had they hiked into the mountains and been absorbed into survivalist compounds? Had they been picked up by the military? Or were they part of those roving packs of Reds circling every city, every neighborhood, in America? Or were they dead? All of them, dead.

As I followed Hunny up the off-ramp my sneakers hit the street in an off-kilter but distinct rhythm and the song from that morning returned.

Way down here. I disappear…

No other lyrics. Just a sad tone and five words.

Hunny dug into the open trunk of a white car, squealed an unintelligible syllable, tucked something into her pocket, and took off again for the drive-thru.

"What did you find?" I asked.

Without answering, she ran ahead into the restaurant.

Being alone for so long had changed me into a cranky old man. Her refusal to respond to a simple question annoyed me like crazy. It occurred to me, leaning on the front window, to leave her there. An easy trick. Turn and hop across the parking lot, swerve around the gas station next door, and head north. Unless she looked out the window in the next ninety seconds, or so, she'd have no idea where I'd gone. I was home free.

No more painful, clingy hugs. No more complaining. No more sharing supplies.

The neighboring gas station wasn't far away. Fifty meters. Maybe seventy-five.

"Hurry up, slow poke," Hunny shouted through the open door.

And I couldn't do it.

She was just a kid. Annoying, sure, but basically helpless. If I abandoned her she'd be dead by morning. And the thought of how much

her parents had loved and cherished her—
enough to send her away to save her life—made
me feel guilty and a little bit responsible. For
their benefit, at least, I could hand her off to
another survivor. If I'd found her and Willa,
there must be others.

So I pushed my way toward the restaurant
even though I'd much rather have stayed on the
road. The stench reached me before I even
cracked the front door, but when I did an
ungodly odor crawled inside my nose like a
living thing.

"Ah." I clapped a hand over my mouth. Too
late. I wouldn't be able to scrub the reeking
smell off me with bleach and steel wool.

Other, not-so-lucky survivors had been
inside this McDonald's before us, and by the
stink, never left. It must have been the first type
of establishment cleaned out during the initial
panic. Searching for helpful supplies was most
likely a complete waste of time.

Five minutes was too long to be stuck in
there.

I wanted to get back on the road and breathe
fresh air again.

But Hunny was thrilled to be anywhere even
slightly reminiscent of her old life. She grinned
as she crossed the dining room and stared up at
the broken menu board as if she considered
making an order.

Except no one was assembling lunch and no

one was frying burgers in the kitchen. That reality was over. For a while, anyway.

"Be quick," I urged, uneasy. "Look for water first and then canned stuff." Even if she only found barbecue sauce and French fry oil, we weren't in any position to be choosy. And if we were really lucky she'd find drinkable water.

The loss of electricity and the vehicles crammed in all around the building like a half-finished blockade made the interior even darker.

The last time I'd been in a McDonald's it had been with my mom and Mason. Dad was a health nut and wouldn't let us eat fast food, but Mom was a French fry junkie and took us every once in a while to a burger joint. Back then the dining room had been crowded and noisy with families, and it had smelled of onions and ketchup.

"Let's hurry," I said, glancing around the shadowy and cavernous interior. "I don't like it here."

Hunny dove over the counter and rifled through cupboards and shelves. "There are a gazillion little bags of nuts and granola and…" Her voice trailed off.

Maybe it had finally sunk in how creepy this place was. Me, I had figured that out the second I smelled it. The whole restaurant gave me the chills. It reminded me too vividly of the way things had been, and how wrecked the world had become.

"Just shove it all in a box or something, and let's go."

"Maya?"

I recognized real fear in her voice, and my heart dropped. She had more than a bad feeling. She was genuinely spooked.

Coming here had been an awful idea.

"Maya," she repeated, "there are bodies back here."

I unsheathed my short sword and swiveled to see all corners of the dining room.

This was even worse than being stuck on the highway in the path of a pack of Reds. There was nowhere to hide. No cover. I was a sitting duck. Sweat blossomed over my entire body as I tensed for the coming fight.

Sometimes infected people created what newscasters had called a nest where they hunkered down and brought food back for prolonged feeding. Food, of course, being other living things. Preferably, human beings. That must've been what was going on behind the counter. We'd stumbled across a zombie's nest. If the zombie was home he'd probably be pretty ticked off.

Images from the action movies Mason had loved flickered through my mind. Throat punches. High kicks. Karate chops. I didn't want to get close enough to a zombie to poke him in the eye, but I might not have a choice. If one attacked Hunny I had to defend her. She couldn't defend herself.

The door to the indoor playground squeaked opened, and I pivoted to face whatever horror stampeded through it.

A little boy no older than seven staggered nearer carrying a pair of yellow, metal tractor toys. He had shaggy brown hair and deep red eyes. The day care sticker on his striped T-shirt read, "Hello, my name is Jack."

He didn't look very terrifying, but so far my good luck juju was on the fritz, so I expected Jack to be the welcoming party for a much more heinous pack. Mama and Papa Zombie maybe? Or an entire death squad of kiddie Reds?

"Hunny," I called. "Stay where you are. There might be more."

She caught sight of little Jack and shrieked, scrambling onto the front counter and doing a nervous dance on her tiptoes.

She'd forgotten how to be quiet, but at least she knew to get to an elevated position.

Taking a cue from her, I sprang onto the nearest table, hip first, and struggled to stand one-legged on the wobbly surface. The table teetered to the left and I spread my arms like a high wire trapeze artist. It worked. Sort of.

Jack didn't have any sympathy for my poor balance. He bared his teeth and ran, full steam, for my position. His bare feet pattered across the tile floor, and then he slammed into my perch. I crumpled to my knees, gripping the table to stay off the floor.

Reds couldn't climb. But they could pull me down.

No matter what else happened I had to stay above him.

Across the room Hunny screamed and screamed, pausing only to suck in huge gulps of air and scream again. The sound of her terror ramped up my own.

Where was Ben? If he barreled through those doors and yanked this kid off me, I would owe him my life twice over. But he didn't show up to save my butt a second time. It was just me and Jack and Hunny. And I wasn't feeling terribly optimistic about our odds.

A buzzing in my ears got louder. The kind of roar a motorcycle made. But it must have been a byproduct of all the fear and adrenalin flushing through my system. I hadn't seen a running vehicle in ages.

If the ferocious first grader heard the buzzing, he didn't let it distract him. He struck my shins with his tractors, their sharp metallic edges biting through my black stretch leggings and drawing blood. Pain ricocheted up my calves and propelled me over tabletops as I tried to decide if it was safer to run and draw the Red away from Hunny or kill him in front of her.

I gripped my sword and waved it in Jack's face, hoping to scare him. He deflected the blade and devastated my ankles with his toys, cutting deep. Dark blood smeared across the table.

The sight of my blood affected him. I expected him to go wild with blood lust like a vampire in a horror film, but instead of growing more agitated, Jack tilted his chin, bringing our faces inches apart. He stared at me. I smelled his foul breath and saw tiny flecks of dried blood on both pale, hollowed cheeks. Maybe I could reason with him. Maybe there was still a spark of humanity inside his little body.

"Jack," I snapped in my crankiest twin sister voice. "Stop it. You're scaring me."

He leaned his face nearer to mine. Little Jack had stained baby teeth in front, and irises a lovely shade of rose. He inhaled deeply, and for a split second I thought he was going to answer me. But he curled his lips over grotesque chompers and, like an irritable Chihuahua, snapped at my nose. I flinched at the last second and saved my face from a major blemish. As in a missing nose or a scarred lip.

Curling my knees up, I kicked him hard in the shoulder. He stumbled back a few steps, readjusted his grip on his tractors, and came at me again with nothing but rage and hunger in his red eyes. Any humanity the child had once possessed was unequivocally missing. Destroyed. *Gone.*

I should have stayed home.

"Kill him!" Hunny screeched, stomping her shoes on the counter. "Kill him, Maya!"

Chapter Six

I raised my sword, and Jack threw his whole weight against the table beneath my feet. My right knee tweaked, I fell, and my sword clattered away. The little kid swung his toy tractors like saw blades and caught me on both arms as I tried to block.

I saw blood. *My* blood.

If I didn't get it together I would end up in the mini monster's nest.

The front door banged open, startling Jack, who turned his attention on the newcomers. Two young men filled the front doorway like an answer to a prayer I hadn't even known I was praying.

A ginger-haired teen stood beside a scruffy, gun-toting blond in a green tee with the words "U.S. Army" stamped across his chest in bold black print. Both had blood on them, but the redhead had three times as much as his buddy. They stared at me, bleeding and gasping on the floor, and were distracted just long enough for little Jack to attack. He swung his tractors at the red-haired boy who kicked Jack in the center of the chest, sending him scuttling back.

Undaunted, Jack steadied himself, growled low in his throat, and sprinted for the men.

The gun went off with a *bang*. Despite only standing five feet from Jack, Army Guy missed the Red entirely. But the sound and smell of gunpowder in the air triggered a whole new panic inside me. So much I couldn't move for a second, couldn't think, couldn't run, couldn't even blink. I watched grayish white smoke curl from the barrel of the weapon, thinking there was no worse sound in the world than the sharp, unsympathetic report of a gun.

My heart sped up as the breath froze in my lungs.

Duck. Hide. *Run*.

I just stared at the handgun as it fired again. And missed again. Finally unable to witness the kill, I ducked my head and slid off the table.

A final shot, a small body dropped, and then silence.

Tears pooled and spilled over both cheeks, which was so stupid. I didn't even know the kid. And two minutes ago he'd been trying to kill me, and I'd considered stabbing him through the chest. But it didn't matter. I cried salty alligator tears, my throat closing up and nearly choking me. Embarrassed by the overreaction, I collected my sword and rushed out the side door, still sobbing.

Maybe it was cruel to cut and run but I had survived this long by staying away from people. Most human beings were dangerous. And firearms were my breaking point.

I got as far as the highway overpass before the guy with the gun, followed closely by Hunny, caught up.

"Maya!" Hunny locked her arms around me and almost knocked me flat.

I didn't have any more patience for her clinging, and I was shaking in my skin. My self-control was long gone.

"Get off me!" I screamed at the top of my lungs, probably attracting every Red for five miles, but my thoughts were scattered leaves after a windstorm. Good God, *he'd fired a gun*.

Mason had fired a single shot at point blank range and killed Mom. I didn't have to witness her murder to loathe guns and the misery they caused.

Hunny refused to let me go. If anything, she tightened her grip, as if she were a wrestler instead of a scared little girl.

The light-haired guy in the green U.S. Army tee approached with his weapon holstered and his hands out like I was a crazy person and needed to be calmed down. I hated him immediately. And yet he was another answer to another prayer.

"Don't leave," he called. "Maybe we can

help each other."

On further inspection these two males were surviving well. They weren't sparkling, but they were decently clean under the fresh blood splatter, which meant they had enough water to bathe. They were doing better than me. I didn't have enough clean fluid to drink.

I'd taken four sponge baths since moving into the panic room behind the kitchen. And those had been at the beginning. I hadn't had enough water to wash with in days.

But the loaded weapon hanging from the guy's belt taunted me. "I don't need any help," I retorted.

"Everybody needs help."

I was doing just fine on my own. Except for the lack of water. And my sprained knee. And the zombie stalking me. But the last thing I needed was this gun nut interfering in my personal life.

"Let go of me, Hunny," I said, calmer, almost robotic. I'd found another survivor. Time to cut my losses and move on. "He's going to take care of you now."

Army Guy rocked back on his heels. "Wait. What?"

Hunny glanced up and, as our eyes met, we had an understanding. I knew what she was searching for. I wasn't her ideal protector. But this guy could be. She unlocked her hands and threw herself around his waist.

I exhaled audibly. It was a huge relief to be free of Hunny and all that responsibility. No more distractions or detours. I was officially alone, exactly the way I preferred it. I was better off on my own. It was simpler. Safer.

With a last wave good-bye, I hobbled away.

"Hold on." The guy pursued me, dragging Hunny. "You can't walk off. It's dangerous out there."

"I've been alone for a long time." Not that it was any of his business.

"I'm Pollard." He flattened one palm against his chest and then extended it for me to shake. "Pollard Datsik. What's your name?"

He had long, blood-flecked fingers. I recalled my dad's rules—don't shake hands, don't touch your face, wash constantly.

I didn't accept his offer. Instead, with my chin up I limped toward the on-ramp to the I–40.

"You're hurt." Pollard trailed me, and Hunny shuffled her feet to keep up, her arms still looped above his hips. "How are you going to protect yourself? All that noise we made will bring out the zombies. You'll be an easy target."

"I'm fine." I stared meaningfully at the loaded weapon on his hip and the blood splatter on his clothing. "I don't need any help."

Joining up with Pollard, the red-haired teen, and whomever else they had in their group would only delay my trip to Dad's lab. Or scrap it altogether.

"Maya," Hunny chimed in, "they saved us from that killer kid. They're cool."

"Fine, they're awesome. But it doesn't matter. I have my own plan."

"You're bleeding," Pollard said. "We have bandages."

I'd almost forgotten about my first zombie fight. Nothing hurt. Yet. But he was right. My sneakers were stained with blood and both my hands were red. I needed first-aid or I might contract an infection at a time I couldn't afford to have a weakened immune system.

"Come with us," he urged. "It's safer in groups."

He was wrong about that. "What do you care?" I asked.

He threw up his hands in defeat. "I'm just trying to keep everyone alive. Have it your way."

As he stalked off, I felt a tickle of panic in my stomach. They had water, a safe place to sleep, and first-aid. I hated to admit it, but I needed them. I couldn't continue in my current state, not alone.

Grumbling, I hopped a step in his direction and that's when I heard them. Zombies in the trees behind the adjacent gas station. A lot of them.

And I was easy prey. "On second thought," I said, gesturing to the approaching pack. "We better get out of here. Trouble's coming."

Pollard recognized the impending danger and hissed, "Russell. Zombies on the move. We're leaving."

Russell came to the door of the restaurant and leaned out. "We haven't collected anything good yet."

There was no other choice and he knew it. "If we don't leave right now we're all going to die. There's not enough ammunition to kill a group that size." Without asking permission, Pollard put an arm around my waist to help me limp faster.

His handgun brushed my ribs, and my pulse p-p-pumped in *tempo presto*. I didn't want to see a gun, let alone hug one.

I believed, like any rational person, that the Reds were ill human beings. Sick, but still people. I didn't go around killing people, let alone kids. It upset me to think of little Jack's body lying inside the restaurant when I knew for a fact a cure existed.

I jabbed my elbow into Pollard's ribs. "Get off me."

He made an *oomph* sound, but tightened his grip, effectively locking my offending arm to my side.

"Shut up, and let me help you," he growled back. "Now, is it just the two of you? Or are there more girls I've gotta save?"

Hunny had no issues trusting strangers whatsoever. "We're totally alone. We don't even have a car." Her eyes lit up. "Do you have a car?"

"Better." Pollard pointed. "I have a dirt bike."

On the sidewalk were parked two Kawasakis with large orange gas cans attached like saddlebags. "We drive up here sometimes looking for fuel."

My heart leapt. "You have a generator?" Did they have real, live electricity?

"We siphon the gas for our bikes. Why?" He narrowed his eyes. "You have something you want to plug in?"

"No." I wasn't ready to share my private business. I couldn't trust them not to take my iPad away. I couldn't even imagine losing my songs. Not to mention photos, videos, text messages…

Pollard released me in order to kick-start one of the dirt bikes. Once he got it running, he glanced up and something over my shoulder caught his attention. "What about him? He's not with you?"

Hunny and I turned at the same time. Ben stood on the other side of the highway. A silent statue between two crumbling concrete barriers.

I stuttered over an appropriate response, but Hunny spoke up with zero difficulties. "He's a Red."

Pollard pulled his weapon, and I bounded forward, slamming the barrel to the side. It fired a bullet into the asphalt only a handful of feet from my right sneaker. But I'd reacted without thinking. I saw a gun and only knew it had to be gotten rid of.

The sound of the gunshot rattled my teeth and liquefied my insides. The lights flickered, but that wasn't right. The sun didn't flicker. And then my vision hazed over as if I was going to cry.

"Are you nuts?" Pollard's face reddened in anger. And maybe a little fear. "Don't ever get in front of my weapon! I almost killed you."

Bile rose, and I bent over a blue two-door to puke. But all I'd had to eat was a couple cookies.

"He's been following us all day," I panted between dry heaves. "He didn't hurt us even when he had the chance."

"A nonviolent Red?" Pollard scoffed. "Are you one of those weirdos who won't kill zombies?"

I didn't like the way he said it, but yes maybe I was. I'd never killed anyone or anything. If that made me a freak, well, so be it.

Hunny waved her arms wildly in the direction of the gas station next door. "Guys!"

Pollard holstered his firearm as Russell emerged from the dining room.

"We need to move. Now." Pollard met my gaze with his shockingly pretty blue eyes. "You're riding with me."

I glanced from the approaching pack of Reds

to Pollard and his mega gun and then back again.

"Why do you have blood on your clothes?" It was an important point. If he didn't give me a believable answer I was out of there.

A shadow flittered across his face. "We were south of here in an auto lube place. We didn't know there were zombies inside until it was too late." His voice cracked. "Russell lost his little sister."

Damn. Swallowing thickly, I avoided his attempts to help and climbed on the back of the Kawasaki.

"The dirt bikes can't carry much more weight." He gestured at my overstuffed backpack. "Dump any non-essentials."

I was afraid if I opened my pack Pollard would get nosy. My personal belongings were none of his business.

"It's all essential."

I sent a last look at Ben where he stood across the lanes of abandoned vehicles, expecting it to be the last time I'd ever see him. It bothered me, losing sight of him. He was a Red zombie. If locked in a room with me, he would tear me to pieces and lick his fingers afterwards.

But he'd saved my life.

I raised my right hand in a silent good-bye. He didn't wave back, but his gaze followed me as Pollard revved the engine, and we took off, zigzagging north on the I–40.

Chapter Seven

Pollard's compound was big and garish and the opposite of my comfortable home in the suburbs.

He and Russell and whoever else was in their group had taken over a super-sized truck stop on the edge of the I–40, the kind with a gas station, car wash, convenience store and a restaurant. A full stop shop.

Knowing Reds couldn't climb, not more than a few steps, Pollard and his crew had pushed various abandoned vehicles into a makeshift wall around the perimeter. And in case that wasn't enough of a deterrent they'd covered all the doors and windows with a hodge-podge of plywood, sheet metal and broken furniture. It was a piecemeal prison. Except it hadn't been barricaded to keep criminals in, but to keep zombies out.

I didn't like it, but my arms and legs had begun to sting during the ten-minute ride, and now all four limbs ached. I needed first aid, and then I'd vanish into the surrounding pines before these two zombie killers even knew I was gone.

Pollard drove me on his dirt bike—Russell and Hunny directly behind on the second bike—up to the entrance. Cold, gray duct tape covered the inside of the front door. Icky. Were they hiding something in there? Or just hiding?

Russell helped Hunny off his bike and then patted his pockets, a frown on his face.

"Everything okay?" Pollard asked his friend, offering his hand to me.

Ignoring his help, I said, "I'm good."

"Sure you are," he grumbled.

Russell checked his pockets one more time. "I lost my lighter." He pulled a pack of cigarettes from his jacket. "It must have fallen out on the ride over." He nodded at Pollard. "Can I borrow yours?"

"Sure." From a pocket, Pollard produced a disposable, tiger print lighter and tossed it.

Besides the green tee Pollard wore cargo pants with bulgy pockets. Anything could be in those compartments. Knives. Ammo. Chloroform. Almost certainly more guns.

Violent types like Pollard always carried more than one weapon. It wouldn't surprise me if he had three or four different handguns hidden on his body. Acid crawled up the back of my throat.

"So weird." Russell shook his head as he

ambled around the side of the building.

I glanced at Hunny, feeling a pattern emerging. The sweet-faced eight-year-old was empty-handed, but at least two things had gone missing around her. Again, I realized I didn't know anything about her except that her parents had been rich and she'd spent time as a glorified prisoner in a medical quarantine.

"I'll help you inside," Pollard said, grabbing my arm without asking and urging me toward the glass doors covered in duct tape. I couldn't see any hint of the interior of the former restaurant and convenience store. Worst-case scenarios ran through my mind. Medical experiment lab? Torture chamber?

My dad would never allow me through that door, especially knowing one of my companions had a firearm and wasn't afraid to use it.

But I needed water, and they had enough to share.

"What's with the tape?" I asked, limping beside him.

"Light attracts Reds." Pollard rapped on the glass door. A distinct knock-knock-knockety-knock. Not a great beat for a soulful country song, but it had its own personality. I might play with the rhythm later, just for fun.

A piece of tape pulled back and an eyeball appeared. Brown, not red. "Pollard?"

"It's me, Simone. Let us in."

A bolt was thrown, and the door opened on

a very non-threatening, twenty-something female with limp brown hair and wide hips.

I exhaled. Not the serial killer I was expecting. Just a normal looking woman.

"Did you fill up?" she asked, swinging the door open. When she spotted Hunny and me, her smile fell away. "Who are they?" Her intelligent brown eyes took in every detail of Hunny's appearance and mine.

"We found them at the McDonald's to the south." He ushered the little girl inside. "They'll have to introduce themselves."

I lingered in the doorway, spying as much as I could of the interior. No visible chains or bone saws, but it was messy with clothes and miscellaneous furniture.

"Hunny Green," my little companion revealed. "She's Maya Solomon."

Good thing we didn't have any real secrets or these people would already know them. Hunny had a big mouth.

"Maya." Pollard gave me a grim smile, and then locked the door behind us. "Make yourselves at home."

They'd redecorated. Most of the tables in the dining room were gone, probably bolted over the windows. The booths had been pushed around and converted into beds strewn with a myriad of blankets and coats.

If I'd thought it was hot and steamy outside, it was sweltering in the cavernous building.

With all the windows sealed shut and no electricity to get a fan moving, the air was warm and heavy. Sweat popped up on my arms and the back of my neck.

While Simone eyed me up and down I slid a few hesitant steps inside. It smelled of sweat and old food, but I couldn't detect any obvious threats. I chanced another step and craned my neck to see around the hostess counter.

I gasped at what I found. Through an archway, the convenience store half of the building was a nirvana of beautiful, pre-packaged, preservative-laden munchies. My mouth opened and stayed that way. Food. Delicious, sugary food. The kind I was almost never allowed to eat.

A lot of it had been consumed, but there were still hundreds of packs of peanuts, cotton candy, potato chips and cereal cups laid out like pirates' treasure on the racks. Sodas, juices and teas were arranged in the shiny glass fridges. I hadn't drunk a soda in months. My dad, being more concerned with health than taste, had only stocked our panic room with water and Gatorade.

The truck stop's drinks would be warm, but I didn't care. I hopped one-legged into the shadowy store, grabbed a can of apple juice from the fridge, popped open the lid, and guzzled it. The sugars hit my stomach hard, and I felt a pang of nausea, but I squelched it and finished the bottle. I couldn't get enough.

The sweet apple scent nearly cleared the earlier, clinging stink of decay from my nose. Almost.

Pollard reached around me and helped himself to a sparkling citrus soda. "Cool, right?"

I couldn't talk through my second bottle of juice, so I just nodded.

"Where is Shelly?" Simone called from the dining room.

Pollard cast me a sad look before answering. "She didn't make it. We were ambushed."

The expression in Pollard's eyes, quickly mirrored in Simone's, brought up a sympathetic rush of emotions in me too. I knew that look and the confusing grief that went with it, the look that said someone you cared about had died without warning.

Simone clutched her shirt over her heart. "Oh, no. Where's Russell?"

Swallowing thickly, I turned my back on their shared grief and hid my reaction by downing a bottle of strawberry flavored water until my stomach bulged at the seams.

"Still outside," Pollard said.

Simone hurried to find him.

"I'm sorry about your friend," I said to Pollard.

"It's not your fault," he said. "We've been inside so many places like that I got overconfident. I messed up rushing in there

89

without a plan. A good soldier always has a plan."

"Are you a soldier?" I asked. That would explain the U.S. Army apparel, but not the crappy shooting skills.

"No." He hung his head. "I was going to enlist, but then…"

Yeah. A lot of things changed when the lights went out and civilization crumbled. I used to have a dad, go to high school, and blog about songwriting. Not anymore.

Hunny jumped around the booths in the dining room in a happy little circle, swinging her arms. "I love this place! I never want to leave!" She dashed past me and raided the convenience store shelves, a joyous ball of energy. Chip bags crinkled and soda caps hissed.

"Help yourselves," Pollard said, and I sensed he was sincere. "We all went a little nuts when we found this place. Don't worry. There's even more stuff piled in the stock room."

"Thanks." But I still didn't trust him or his two friends. Not when they were so quick to pull the trigger.

From the outside Mason hadn't looked like a murderer. Cal hadn't looked like a sadist and a bully.

Pollard, Russell, and Simone seemed like good enough people to leave Hunny with, though. She was pro-gun.

"Let's get you off your feet." Pollard

gestured toward the booths in the next room, and I hopped over and stretched out my sore legs on a bench. Keeping his eyes averted, he wadded a sweater into a pillow and stuffed it under my right foot. My leg felt immediately better.

"Thanks." I twisted, taking in more details of the truck stop. Nothing screamed danger. All I saw was mess and clothes and some empty water bottles. But I was no longer comfortable around other people. I couldn't completely relax.

He inspected the cuts on my shins, moving my torn black leggings up to see better. Little Jack's metal tractors had cut bloody crisscross lines into my legs. I leaned forward to help clean them.

"What happened to you guys?" Pollard asked.

"The boy in the McDonald's." I didn't say, *The boy you killed*, but I thought it. There had been other options than shooting Jack. I'd survived as long as they had and never hurt anyone. I hated that he'd pulled a gun first and asked questions...*never*.

"We have first aid. Can I clean these cuts and put bandages on them?"

"Uh." Overwhelmed by so many new people, I didn't know how to politely say I'd rather be alone for a few minutes, but my exhaustion gave me the excuse I needed. "Can I rest first? I've been on my feet all day."

"Oh, yeah." He jerked to his full height of near six feet. "Do you want a blanket or something?" Without waiting for an answer he snapped open a fuzzy afghan and dropped it over my hips. "Make yourself at home." He left in a rush.

I didn't sleep, but the garbled voices coming from outside, the security of the barricades, and the warm air lulled me into a hazy daydream. I curled up and fantasized I was home in my own bed and not injured in a hot, sort of sour smelling truck stop surrounded by strangers.

With my eyes closed, I imagined my white ceiling and lavender walls. I could see my dresser and all the stuff spread over the top, every piece of it important to me. A guitar-shaped porcelain dish where I kept my earrings. A miniature bottle of perfume I wore on special occasions. Painted clay frogs I'd made in ninth grade art class. I could practically smell the carpet and feel the soft cotton sheets embracing me.

Someday I would go back. After I got to Raleigh, found my dad's lab, and liberated his cure to the 212R virus. I pictured myself, a little older and wiser, packing a bag and setting off along a road alone, headed home to Cherry Blossom Court.

I heard a tiny clinking sound and turned my head in time to catch Hunny sliding shiny quarters into her dirty socks.

"What in the world are you doing?"

Chapter Eight

Hunny startled wildly, a sure sign of guilt as far as I was concerned. She must have thought I was dead asleep and she was in the clear to steal things.

"Nothing." She snapped upright. "What?"

"Where did you get those? The cash register?" It wasn't taking money, now worthless anyway, that irritated me. It was the stealing and sneaking and lying. "Is my clicker pen in there? And Russell's lighter? What else do you have?"

I pushed myself to my feet as Pollard entered through a swinging door from the kitchen. He'd washed the blood splatter off his arms and face and it improved his appearance tenfold.

"You're up." He grinned at me, and as his expression warmed he appeared younger than ever. Not that much older than me.

Hunny ran and threw herself at Pollard, her arms circling his waist. "She's being mean to me."

Ha. I snorted, surprised she wasn't already giving the man her pretty pouty face.

He tried to disentangle himself, but Hunny held on like a monkey. Finally, he looked at me for help. "What happened?"

I didn't give Hunny time to run off or tell a story about how it was all my fault. I yanked up the back of her shirt. She had a Barbie in a puke green ball gown and a TV remote jammed under the waistband of her jeans. She thrashed, but I was quick and emptied both her front pockets. A lighter, a wristwatch, a banana flavored lollipop and a beaded hair clip clattered to the floor. If I could have bent down on my injured leg and removed her shoes and socks I'd have done that too because I had a feeling there was more hiding in there than quarters.

Squeezing Pollard, Hunny wept noisily. "Don't be mad at me," she sobbed into his T-shirt. "I'm sorry. I'm sorry!"

"Unbelievable." I sighed. "You don't have to steal. Everything's free now." It didn't make sense in my brain.

What was the point of sneaking around stealing stuff? What kind of rush did she get from dead people's things? The rules were different now. It wasn't like anyone was going to arrest her for shoplifting. So, why do it at all?

I was reminded, again, that I knew next to nothing about any of these people.

"You stole Russell's lighter?" Pollard asked above the crying. He just kept shaking his head, looking as flabbergasted as I felt. "What for? There's at least two dozen on the front counter."

Hunny cried louder.

The high-pitched noise set me even further on edge. I palmed the handle of my short sword, waiting for Pollard's reaction. With his itchy trigger finger I feared he'd have an equally hot temper. I had dealt with bullies before.

"Let go of me," Pollard said gently. "No one's mad at you. I'm just surprised is all."

Simone and Russell, attracted by the noise, walked in through the kitchen. I watched to see how they would respond. I hadn't seen Russell fire a gun at the McDonald's, and Simone wasn't obviously packing heat, but that didn't mean they both weren't violent gun nuts with pistols under their shirts.

Russell immediately spotted his recovered property.

"Cool, where did you find my lighter?" He picked it up and flicked the wheel. A tiny flame burst to life.

"Never mind," Pollard grumbled. Because Hunny wouldn't let go, he finally lifted her right off her feet and set her on a chair. She tried one last time to latch onto Pollard, but he carefully avoided her clutches.

"Listen," he barked, silencing the entire room. I flinched at the harsh tone of his voice.

But then his words quieted and his expression softened. "We're a team here, you got it? And if you're going to be part of our team, know that we don't steal from each other. We help each other. We share and compromise and protect each other. If you want something, then ask." He folded his arms. "Understand?"

And they listened to him. Everyone consented, even Hunny. Though Simone was clearly the oldest member of the little group, Pollard was in charge. I glanced from Russell to Simone. They looked up to Pollard. Either he had qualities worth respecting or he was some cult leader. People looked up to them too.

Hunny, red-faced and hiccupping, nodded.

"Do you understand?" he asked again.

"I understand."

"Now apologize to Russell, and we'll forget this ever happened."

In the tiniest voice possible, Hunny apologized, and the tension in the room eased.

The little girl found a quiet spot behind a magazine stand to nurse her wounded pride, and Simone and Russell strolled into the store area.

Though she was embarrassed now, Hunny would do well here. These people seemed decent. They could keep her fed and safe and maybe even convince her to brush her tangly hair. I felt good about the decision to continue my journey as soon as I could walk without falling down.

"Ready for that first aid?" Pollard asked me.

I wiggled my toes. The dried blood pulled and itched. "Yeah, that'd be really nice."

Pollard collected a cardboard box stuffed with alcohol, cotton balls, antibiotic cream and dozens of standard size Band-Aids. And he had a handgun holstered on his hip.

I pictured the thing going off inside the McDonald's.

He caught me staring. "You don't like guns?"

That was an understatement. "No."

"It's for self defense. I only use it when I have to." He sat beside me on the bench. "Roll up your pants."

Like it was no big deal. *Just roll up your pants.* But as I slowly exposed my legs to him, the warm, stale air of the truck stop diner tickled my calves, and it felt like a big deal. Like getting undressed.

"How old are you?" I blurted out, keeping my eyes on my knees. That felt safer because Pollard was suddenly far into my personal space.

"Nineteen. You?"

I chanced a look at Pollard and was thrown off guard by how blue his eyes were. "Seventeen."

"You were going to start your senior year in the fall?" he guessed.

I was. Until the world went topsy-turvy. "Exactly."

"My senior year was fun," Pollard said, unscrewing the bottle of rubbing alcohol. "I miss it."

"High school?" Weren't people always relieved to finish high school?

"No. The old world."

Well, I missed my old life, too. Plenty. But that world was gone, and by the look of things—forever. I was more interested in the new communities we could build after my dad's elixir took effect.

Pollard set the bottle of rubbing alcohol beside me and counted out fluffy cotton balls. I reached for the medicine, unused to people doing things for me.

"I'll do it."

The corner of his mouth compressed. "Will you just relax and let me help you?"

What he didn't seem to understand was, I couldn't calm down. Even my fingers were twitchy. Too much isolation, maybe. Or too much excitement in the last twenty-four hours. But short of ripping the materials out of his hands, I had no choice.

He laid an old shirt under my legs before pouring the alcohol directly onto my gnarly looking cuts. It stung like crazy. I tapped my feet in a quick, country two-step rhythm. Tuppa-tuppa-tuppa-tap.

"Sorry." Pollard dabbed at the blood with cotton balls. "Does it hurt?"

"Mmm." *A lot.*

"It'll keep it from getting infected."

Thanks to my dad I knew all about sanitation and infection. If I'd thought of packing first aid when I left my home the day before I wouldn't have been there. I would have been in downtown Raleigh. I vowed to never take off without emergency supplies again. Huge rookie mistake.

He poured another stream of rubbing alcohol over the worst cut, burning a trail of fire down my calf and wetting my socks. More than ever I needed a shower. A long hot shower with body wash and a loofah. I flopped back onto the booth and covered my eyes with both hands. But those days were long gone. The best I could hope for was a sponge bath or a dip in a bug-infested creek.

I missed the sweet-smelling personal hygiene products of the past. Bubblegum body wash. Peppermint hand lotion. Coconut conditioner. After the apocalypse one of the first things I was putting on my to-do list was recreating scented soap.

Pollard laid his palm on my good knee, and it was a solid reassuring weight. "Are you all right?" His fingers squeezed lightly. "You're not going to pass out or anything are you?"

I didn't move a muscle. I was too afraid he'd

leave his hand there, and at the same time afraid he'd take it away. No one had touched me kindly in a long time. And Hunny's clinging hugs didn't count. Not really.

"I'm not going to pass out."

He removed his fingers and dabbed some more with the cotton balls. "Where did you come from?"

Thinking about my history helped me forget the sting below my knees. "Charlotte, originally," I answered. "But two years ago we moved to Parrish Meadows, a suburb a couple miles south of here." When my family burst and splintered, leaving my dad and me on our own.

The easiest thing for Dad to do at the time, because neither of us could live in the old house without having coinciding nervous breakdowns, was sell the house I'd grown up in, pack the belongings that didn't hurt too much to touch, and go somewhere brand new. A house with no history, no past, and no secrets.

It hadn't solved all our problems, but the new house on Cherry Blossom Court had helped me feel closer to my old self.

"What about you?" I countered, meeting his blue eyes again.

"I started college last year in Louisville."

As he bent over my legs, his blond hair obscured his eyes. I had the insane desire to brush it out of his way.

"When everyone started getting sick," he

continued, "I drove home. But the roads were so bad it took me a week to drive to Durham. *A week*. And I only stopped when I absolutely had to." He groaned as if it still aggravated him. "I talked to my family on the phone the whole way. They all had fevers, my sister Opha the worst." Pollard replaced the alcohol in the box and searched for bandages. "But then they stopped answering my calls. When I finally got home they were gone, and it was clear what had happened."

I felt a pang of sympathy. "I'm sorry," I said. "I lived with my dad too. Before things got bad."

Pollard bobbed his head. "Is Hunny your sister, then?" he asked.

That was a stretch. We didn't look anything alike. She had short, blonde curls and I had my mom's straight, glossy black hair. "No. She and I ran into each other yesterday. The lady who was taking care of her was killed. So I let her follow me around." But that was over. As far as I was concerned, Hunny was Pollard's problem now. He just didn't know it yet.

He spread antibiotic cream over my each of my scrapes, and I flinched at his unexpected touch. The two jagged, still oozing cuts on my left leg were just as deep as the defensive wounds on my forearms. And every one of them stung.

"Does that hurt?" he asked.

"A little." I sat up. More than anything the

feel of his fingers on my bare flesh unsettled me. "Thanks for taking us in." They had saved our butts back in that drive-thru. I owed him and Russell a lot. If they hadn't burst in, I might be dead. Hunny too.

"We need to stick together." He smoothed a bandage onto my leg, and then another and another. "There aren't many people left."

"Have you seen anyone else?" I asked, perking up.

Pollard blew out a long stream of breath. "It's been a while. Finding you and Hunny was definitely a surprise."

That's what I'd been afraid of. How would I ever locate a doctor to replicate my dad's cure if there weren't any uninfected people left? I knew a lot of stuff, just from living with a chemist and volunteering at a hospital, but there was no way I could read the formulas, analyze the chemicals, and create new batches. I might as well try to build a rocket ship out of trash from the parking lot dumpster.

"But Russell and Simone are good people," Pollard continued. "You'll see."

Probably not since I was leaving first chance I got, but I didn't argue. "How do you know them?"

"I didn't before the plague, but we've become like family since grouping up. It's been over a week, I guess. Russell and Shelly—" he cleared his throat, "were hiding on the roof of a grocery store. Russell's a good kid. A little immature, but he's only fifteen. He'll grow."

"And Simone?"

He cracked a smile. "I searched the police station on Jefferson for ammo and I found her locked in a cell. They'd arrested her for public intoxication, and then left her there with a sandwich and a cup of coffee."

"Oh." Mason had been in a juvenile detention center when the red virus struck. Had he been locked in a cell and forgotten? Had he died of dehydration and rotted in his bunk? God, I hoped not. I hoped there had been a riot and he'd escaped. Even if I never saw him again, I wanted to believe he was out there in the world. Alive.

"Simone was very, *very* happy to see me." He rested his hand on my knee for the briefest moment, his blue eyes twinkling. "Take it easy, okay? I'll go put this stuff away."

I smiled despite the exhaustion creeping up on me.

While he packed the first aid kit, I rested flat on the bench and closed my eyes. But I felt too vulnerable to sleep around a group of strangers. The truck stop's exits were sealed. It would be so easy to go from guest to prisoner in a place like this.

Maybe it had been a mistake grouping up with them, even temporarily. Teaming up with other survivors was the last thing I needed to be doing. I wish I'd been clear-headed enough at the McDonald's to walk away. But the gunshots and little Jack and the blood and Ben stalking me had all messed with my emotions and my logical thinking.

Hunny slithered into the dining room and, with eyes averted, crawled into my lap. I sat up and lightly finger-combed her blonde curls, thinking how pretty they'd look clean and tangle-free. Like doll's hair.

"I'm sorry I stole your pen." She produced my Hello Kitty ballpoint from up her sleeve and offered it to me.

Huffing a laugh, I shook my head. "If you'd asked me I probably would have given it to you. I only keep it so I can write songs, but I haven't been able to write since the red virus." Except for that sad snippet of an elegy that had come to me on the highway. And I couldn't bear to finish it.

Hunny clicked the pen up and down, up and down. "What kind of songs?"

"Country music," I said. "That's my favorite."

"Can you sing one of your songs for me?"

My stomach clenched. I wrote music, but I wasn't a great singer. I heard melodies and riffs and beats and hooks in my head, but my voice couldn't capture all the nuances I dreamed about. I'd given up any fantasy of having a singing career a couple years earlier. I would have been happy songwriting full time and letting the pros handle the vocals.

"I don't sing," I told her. "But I want you to do something for me."

"What?"

"Stop stealing from survivors. The whole world is one big free-for-all. You don't have to steal from me or any of these other people."

She tucked her head under my chin and mumbled, "I want things. I used to have a lot of things."

Like a warm, wiggly puppy she curled into my body heat, and my arms instinctively circled her. I inhaled the scent of her hair, a stray curl tickling my nose. Mom used to hold me on her lap. I'd been an idiot to take her hugs and kisses for granted.

"Yeah." I wanted stuff too. I wanted my family back and my guitar and electricity. I wanted clean water to flow when I turned on a faucet and fresh food and movies and music. I wanted it all.

I might actually get my wish if I found my dad's cure. But I'd never get there sitting around daydreaming.

"Go pick out a drink for me, will you?"

Hunny gave me a last squeeze and ran into the store section of the building. I stood and tested my knee. It was starting to hurt again, but the scrapes on my arms and ankles felt much better. I pushed my leggings down and shook blood back into my feet.

I hadn't arrived at the truck stop with much. I unzipped my bag and double-checked its contents. Before I left I needed to re-pack. Out there on the road a first aid kit would be crucial. And I could use a hat or a pair of nice sunglasses. Plus a couple lighters to make fire. A can opener. Lip balm…

But I had to have water. As much clean water as I could carry.

I swung my backpack off the ground, slipped it onto my shoulders, and hooked my sword through a belt loop. My worldly possessions had been reduced to what I could carry in my hands, and the thought devastated me. Maybe Hunny wasn't so crazy after all. I wanted all the things that had once made me happy, too.

I found a slit in the tabletop over the front window and stared at the eerily still parking lot beyond.

Not that long ago the commercial property had been a noisy, crowded stop for tourists and truckers. If I concentrated I could pick up faint remnants of bacon grease, grilled ground beef, and barbeque sauce. The truck stop's managers had probably played music, too. Popular, catchy songs with upbeat melodies. The gas pumps would've been running nonstop, and the clerk would've been swiping credit cards all day through the cash register while truckers and tourists ambled along the aisles.

Now the unrelenting humid heat of late spring made everything smell stale and slightly rotten. With no background noise except the wind and the birds, every sound, from a footstep to an insect crossing the floor, was amplified. And everything that had been so important a couple months ago lay abandoned and quiet and forgotten.

I had to start over. With my dad's elixir, I had to create a new world for the living. For people like Ben and the countless other lost souls wandering the earth. Because I might be the only person left who could.

"Going somewhere?"

Chapter Nine

I spun from the boarded up window and found Pollard, flanked by Russell and Simone, waiting expectantly for an answer. Hunny ran over, shoved a bottle of warm Sprite into my hands, and—opportunist that she was—flung her arms around Pollard's waist. He patted her back once, and then forced her off. She didn't wander far, though.

Going somewhere? *Absolutely.* As quickly as possible. "Yes. Raleigh." If I didn't leave soon I was afraid I never would.

"Bad idea," Russell said, slouching into a booth. "It's crawling with Reds."

"We're safer here," Simone said. "We're protected."

"I know, but—"

Pollard spoke over me. "You're hurt. Wait a day or two until you're stronger. If you go out there now you'll be like a wounded kitten in front of a pack of wild dogs."

"Nice imagery." I put weight on my right

knee and winced. I didn't want to stay and get stuck, but I wasn't suicidal, either.

"You can sleep here tonight," Pollard continued. "Eat. Rest. Take whatever you need."

The truth was I was hungry and dehydrated. The cuts on my arms and legs stung. My sprained knee throbbed. And Hunny still hadn't brushed her hair. A decent meal and a good night's sleep could make the difference between reaching my dad's lab and failing.

"Okay," I conceded. "One night."

"Good." Pollard exhaled. "Then let me show you around. Maybe I can convince you to stay longer."

Unless he had a 212R antiserum of his own tucked behind the cookie display, I couldn't stay.

He stretched out a hand, and it was on the tip of my tongue to say, *No, thank you*. I didn't know anything about him except he was a wannabe soldier, a crap shot, and he grew up in Durham.

But he stood there staring at me with soft blue eyes, looking young and kind. Normal. Safe. He'd kept his gun holstered. He'd fixed my cuts. He'd welcomed us into his makeshift fortress.

"Sure." I accepted his hand and followed him down a short, shadowy hallway leading to bathrooms and a utility closet. At the end, he kicked open a step ladder and climbed through a panel in the ceiling.

For a moment he disappeared onto the roof, and I leaned uncertainly against the wall. If he expected me to scamper after him, he was out of luck. My bad knee stranded me on the ground floor.

Maybe he could describe whatever was up there?

But like a good little soldier, Pollard had a plan. He reached both hands toward me. "I've got you," he assured.

Sucking in a deep breath, I stepped up on my good leg and clasped his hands. As if I weighed no more than a sleeping bag, he pulled me up beside him.

It took me a second to get my footing, but when I did I needed a little space to breathe. He was too close. Too tall. Too male. Pretending a fascination with a satellite dish, I put distance between us.

"I wanted you to see what a perfect location we've got here." Pollard pointed to the trees around the rear of the truck stop property. "It's a lot sweeter than it looks from the inside. There are plenty of animals in the woods to hunt. There's a stream about three-quarters of a mile that way." He looked north toward Raleigh. "There are enough businesses and residences within walking distance to stock our storeroom. We're close to the highway to siphon fuel from parked cars. And we've put a lot of work into securing the ground floor. If we're quiet and keep the windows covered the Reds walk right past us." He glanced at me. "You and Hunny will be safe here."

Not me. I wasn't staying. Besides, my home was on Cherry Blossom Court and nowhere else. "Hunny will love it," I agreed. "But I have to keep moving."

His brows drew together. "Maya, I'm trying to restore the old world here," he said, and his eyes shone with determination. "You could be part of that."

I poked at the satellite dish, and it wobbled on its stand. "You miss the old world," I guessed.

Pollard chuckled in surprise. "Don't you?"

"Yeah, of course." Sometimes I felt like I might drown in the feelings of loss I had for my former life. I ached inside for my family and my home and all the people we'd lost. It wasn't a lack of emotion that was my problem. If anything, it was the opposite. Depression had kept me in my home when I probably should have traveled to Raleigh sooner.

I wandered further away. Pollard's group hadn't simply redecorated downstairs. They'd changed things up there too. A pop-up canopy shaded a couple camping chairs. It was a lot cooler under the canvas than inside the building. Maybe they spent hot afternoons in the shade, enjoying cool breezes and warm sodas. It sounded a lot nicer than crouching in my panic room, sweating through my clothes, alone and thirsty. Maybe Pollard and his groupies were on to something.

On the other side of a large metal structure someone had printed "SOS" in huge letters across the roof in white paint. I craned my neck to see the crystalline blue sky above. Not a cloud in sight, let alone an aircraft. Who did he think would see his plea for help?

A little further exploration uncovered four identical backpacks lined up under an AC unit along with a blue plastic tub and four gallons of fresh water. The furthest pack had the name "POLLARD" drawn on it in black Sharpie.

I nudged his backpack with the toe of my sneaker. "Pollard, huh? How did you get that name?"

He squinted as if he saw right through my evasion, sighed, and then joined me at the edge of the SOS message. "My dad loved everything about the military. Twenty years in the army wasn't enough. He spent two weekends a month with Civil War re-enactors and named me after the hero Captain Jessup Pollard of the 101st Illinois Cavalry," he recited.

"Were you related to the guy?"

"Distant cousins."

As far as I knew my name hadn't held any great significance for my parents. They'd loved the way it sounded, but now that I thought about it, maybe I was lucky my dad hadn't named me Galadriel.

"Ever go by Paul or anything like that?" Pollard was a heavy name to pin on a little kid. I wasn't sure I could have handled it.

"My dad wouldn't let me have a nickname. He said it was disrespectful." He shrugged. "Now, I can't imagine going by any other name."

"Your dad sounds like a tough guy."

Pollard kicked at leaves and debris as he fiddled with a vent on the AC unit. He didn't answer, but he didn't need to. I got the gist.

"How long have you been here?" I asked, unzipping the first backpack. It was a mishmash of matches, cooking oil, and water purification tablets. My emergency backpack would be organized way differently. In my opinion, a can of chili was more important than all the corn oil in the world. And where was his can opener?

"Weeks." He shooed me away and zipped the bag closed. "Like I said, you'll be safe here. We want to build up our numbers and then take over an even larger area. A whole strip mall maybe. Or a hotel. Gather more survivors and make the place as close to what it used to be as we can."

Something in the distance, something near the gas pumps, caught my eye. A figure. I crossed the roof to see it more clearly.

Ben stood, chest heaving, between two abandoned semi-trucks looking exactly as I remembered him. Navy blue work clothes. Heavy leather boots. Dirty black hair. He must have run for miles to catch up to us.

As if sensing me, he lifted his red eyes to mine.

"Do you know that guy?" Pollard asked, his elbow bumping my arm.

I tensed, feeling protective of Ben. He'd saved me once, and I owed him.

"No." Hunny hadn't either or she would have said so a long time ago. She couldn't keep a secret to save her life. "Maybe he knows me, though." It might explain why he continued to follow us. He could've gone to my high school or lived in my subdivision. It was impossible to tell while he was in his currently filthy, zombified state. But he didn't look familiar.

"How long has he been tracking you?"

"More than a day."

Pollard's voice jumped an octave. "He's been hunting you for a whole day?"

If Ben had been hunting me he would have killed me already. I thought of his hands on the tree branch beside my feet. And his rough fingers on my arm. A hunter didn't behave that way with its prey.

"He's not hunting me. He just watches." I turned on Pollard. "Promise me you won't shoot him." He could probably hit Ben from the roof with a rifle, though the way Pollard shot, maybe not. "Please."

"Why do you care so much?"

Was he serious? "Because he didn't hurt us." Even when it was in his best interest. "He's not being aggressive."

Pollard opened his mouth, closed it, and finally shook his head. "I can't promise that."

Unacceptable. Re-building the human civilization had to include Reds, too. Ben was just as much a person as I was. "You talk about protecting people. What makes him any different?"

His expression hardened. "He's not a real person. He's dangerous."

"He's sick."

"Holy crap, you've really got a soft spot for that thing, don't you?" He tossed up both hands. "Okay. I give up. As long as he stays over there I won't shoot him."

"Thank you." I laid my hand on his bicep, warm and firm beneath his green tee, and then blushed because I couldn't believe I'd touched him at all.

"Come on," he said, nodding toward the hatch. "It's almost dinner time." At the access panel, Pollard offered both his hands. When I hesitated, he said, "Trust me."

I wanted to.

I placed my hands in his.

As soon as my feet were back on solid ground I rushed through the hallway and toward the sound of people. Hunny slouched on a booth beside an open bag of nacho flavored chips, her belly round and distended from all the junk she'd inhaled. Russell was whispering to Simone near the cash register, but hushed when he spotted me.

"Will you help me with dinner?" Pollard asked, appearing right behind me.

I frowned. "Uh." I didn't want to be rude, but I needed a breather.

Pollard got off on being the boss. I hadn't had anyone in charge of me for a while, and I wasn't looking for a new guardian.

"I want to show you how we do things," Pollard added.

I wouldn't mind more of the grand tour, just to see how other survivors handled the new challenges of a post-plague world. My dad hadn't exactly left me with a lot of survival knowledge.

"Okay."

The truck stop kitchen was big and full of modern appliances, now mostly useless. What good was an industrial-sized fryer when the electricity was off?

Pollard had gone caveman on the place and built a fire pit in the big sink and topped it with a rigged spit and a BBQ grill. Wood, newspaper, and lighter fluid were piled on the floor. Six fuzzy, ground squirrels slumped on the stainless steel counter.

I hadn't seen fresh meat in so long my eyes

popped. I was no hunter. A gatherer, for sure, but not once a hunter. "Where did you get these?"

"I caught them."

"How?"

"I made snares." He wiped sweat from his brow with his sleeve. "I told you the woods are full of animals."

He glanced once at my bad leg and pulled a chair over, gesturing for me to sit.

"Can you show me how?" I asked, sinking gratefully into the seat.

"Sure. In the morning?"

"No. Now." I smiled at his look of confusion. "If it's okay. I want to try to catch some by morning."

Reds craved meat. Even Reds following my trail to save my skin from a hungry pack. If that Red ate an animal it might curb his appetite for larger prey. Namely, me.

"What about your knee?"

"It's better," I fibbed. If anything, it hurt worse, but I refused to let it stop me.

"If you're sure." He tossed a towel on top of the six skinny corpses. "I'll fix these later. Let's go now before it gets too late."

I grinned in anticipation. I'd never learned any survival tricks beyond opening cans of tuna with a crank and rationing supplies. Not once had Dad mentioned what to do if I ventured out into the world in search of fresh meat or clean water.

"We'll head into the forest," Pollard said, quickly packing a bag. "I have traps not too far from here I can show you."

On our way through the dining room I snapped my fingers at Hunny and then finger-spelled, "*B-e b-a-c-k s-o-o-n.*"

She rolled her eyes at me, but close to her belly she signed, "*O-K.*"

Pollard unlocked the front door, checked that the parking lot was clear, and then led the way outside into almost unbearable heat. I missed air conditioning. And swimming pools. And ice cream cones. I was sweating through my shirt by the time I'd hobbled through the automobile barrier.

Without saying a word, Pollard pulled me tight to his side, taking some of my weight and making it easier to walk. His proximity made me even hotter and stickier, though. I walked easier, but I wasn't sure it was worth the increased body temp. Pressed up against him, I tried to ignore how tall and solid he was.

The forest loomed darkly ahead, and I got a bad feeling in my stomach. My instincts warned me to stay away from the woods. Dangerous animals lurked between the trees.

"Ever see any wild dogs out here?" I asked, checking over my shoulder. "Or other carnivores?"

"Every once in a while. But if I fire into the

air they run away. So far, they've never bothered me."

"It's weird." I was chattering, but couldn't stop. "It doesn't seem like 212R infected animals, but they've gone wild anyway. Same difference, I guess. They still want to kill us."

Pollard frowned at me. "Did you have a bad experience with an animal?"

"Dogs chased us this morning. They didn't actually bite us, but it was close."

"Don't worry," he assured with a confident smile. "I'll keep you safe."

By the time we trudged past the gas pumps my clothes stuck to me with sweaty glue.

Movement near the abandoned semi-trucks caught my eye. Ben shuffled three steps in our direction. My free arm gripped Pollard's waist tight to prevent him from doing anything stupid.

I shook my head at Ben, sending him a silent plea with my eyes to wait and not follow us.

Pollard had promised me on the truck stop roof to show restraint, despite carrying a gun on his hip, but I still didn't trust him not to hurt Ben.

The Red paused beside a Mack truck and stayed there. Pollard guided me into the dense pines beyond the parking lot, and I lost sight of Ben.

We crunched through dry grass and weaved around scrub brush, but the temperature was more manageable in the shade of the trees, and I slipped out from under Pollard's arm. Off balance, he faltered in a nest of dry pine needles, but caught himself and then threw me an exasperated look.

"Anyway," he said. "The trick, or what my dad taught me, is to set up the snare so it breaks the animal's neck as it gets yanked into the air." He hopped over a fallen tree and held out his hand to help me. Without thinking, I accepted it.

Holding hands. Skin to skin contact. My dad would've had a fit.

A narrow grassy clearing appeared between the pines.

"This is one of the places I set traps." He knelt beside a scraggly tree.

Only when I hunched down beside him did I see a noose attached to a stick in the ground, its tip tied to a branch above it with silver wire.

"It's all about tension," Pollard said, coming close to touching the trap, but not quite. "Have you ever killed an animal?"

I shook my head. I'd never killed anything. All my life my food had come from the grocery store or a restaurant. For the past two weeks I'd been living off canned and bagged food. My outdoor survival knowledge was nil.

"We don't have much time before it gets dark." Pollard unpacked his little bag and lined up a rubber mallet, a knife, a handheld saw, and a coil of what looked like piano wire.

I picked up the line and tested its weight.

Very light, but strong. "Where did you get all this?"

"It took a while." He broke a branch off a nearby tree. "But I knew I'd eat if I set snares. Here." He handed me the gnarled branch. "You have to saw it in half."

I pressed hard, and the saw chewed into the fresh wood. It didn't match his at all.

"Make the notches like this." He guided my strokes with his long, rough fingers, demonstrating how to dig the saw's teeth into the hard wood and create linking indentations on each half of the branch. When he released me I nervously wiped both palms down my thighs.

My first attempt at an animal trap was way amateur, but he didn't laugh. Instead, he fixed the notches with a couple slashes of his pocketknife so they interlocked. Then he tied the wire, buried one end of the stick, and planted the snare in the dark, sandy soil a few feet from his.

It wouldn't be pretty, but I'd be able to set one by myself if I had to.

"We'll check for animals in the morning. I usually have something for dinner every day."

"Your dad taught you how to hunt?" It astounded me that people still knew how to do things like that. My family—for generations— and I had been thoroughly citified. Before tonight, I couldn't have trapped an animal if I had a month and an arsenal.

"He was real outdoorsy," Pollard said. He shouldered his bag and then slipped an arm around my waist to help ease the pain in my right leg. "Your dad wasn't?"

I couldn't control a snort of laughter. He talked for hours about Tolkien's style and themes and sources, but he didn't know a snare from a jump rope. In fact, he was more likely to get caught in a snare than to build one.

"Not at all," I assured. "He was a PhD. A nerd."

"My dad was a survivalist nut. He was always afraid of the government collapsing so he learned to live off the land." Pollard gazed into the distance at his truck stop citadel. "I guess, in a way, he was right."

"Well," I said, "it's a good thing he showed you as much as he did, huh?"

"Yeah." He didn't sound too grateful. "Lucky."

As we passed the gas pumps in the lavender dusk my gaze shifted automatically to the last spot I'd seen Ben. He hadn't moved. *Astonishing.* What had interested him so strongly he couldn't walk away from it? There was nothing here for him besides living flesh, which he could get in a hundred other places around town. So, why was he here?

Something on the pavement, a squiggle of color that didn't belong, caught my eye. Curious, I got close enough to see what appeared to be writing. Another SOS maybe.

I deciphered my name and my chest constricted as I quickened my pace to read the entire message.

Mason,

I can't forgive you, but I still love you.

Maya

"That wasn't here yesterday," Pollard said, trailing me. "What is it?"

I couldn't say it aloud. It was too painful.

I remembered the exact moment I'd scribbled the note on the back of one of my school photos from the beginning of the year and mailed it to my brother in juvenile detention in a care package at Christmastime.

"I don't understand," I mumbled, scanning the surrounding area.

Ben loomed near the diesel gas pumps, fifty yards away, but even at that distance I detected the faint mist of white paint on his navy shirt.

"Did you do this?" Pollard pressed, suspicion darkening his blue eyes.

"No." I gestured at Ben. "He did."

Pollard's frown deepened. "I don't understand what's going on."

I don't either. "I wrote this in a note to my brother." I thought back to the most painful time in my life. "Over Christmas. Almost six months ago." Because right after his incarceration I was in too much pain to write, but after months and months of grieving both Mom's death and his

124

arrest I sent him the message.

"Then how did it get *here*?"

"Ben must have my picture." My skin tingled unpleasantly. "There's no other explanation."

Pollard crouched and tested the paint. "He's trying to communicate with you."

But how had he found my picture?

Pollard added, "He's not like the others, is he?"

"No." I stared across the lot at Ben and then instinctively took a step in his direction.

Pollard grabbed hold of my upper arm. "You're still not getting any closer. He's infected. He's dangerous."

"But—"

"He can't answer your questions anyway." He dragged me away, off balance, but I didn't struggle because my thoughts were muddier than any riverbank. If I sent my picture to Mason, how had it ended up in a zombie's possession?

I didn't know the answer, yet, but I was afraid when I learned the truth it wouldn't be pleasant.

Knock-knock-knockety-knock. After a moment, Russell unlocked the front door and let us in.

"Let's finish making dinner," Pollard said, dumping his bag on the floor amid the mess in the dining room.

I checked on Hunny, who was playing cards with Simone, and then followed him into the kitchen, but my concentration was shattered. I hoped he didn't need too much help in prepping the meal because I'd be useless.

Why didn't Mason have my picture? How had Ben found it?

I dragged my feet into the kitchen. The six squirrel corpses were right where we'd left them. I pointed at the row of dead vermin as an idea occurred to me. "Can I have one?"

"I'll cook them up. They'll be ready to eat in a while."

"Can I have one now?"

"They're raw."

"I know. Can I?"

He nodded, but added, "You'll get sick."

He assumed it was for me, and that was fine. He wouldn't approve of my idea anyway. So let him think I liked raw flesh.

"Thank you." Slightly grossed out at the dead thing, I snatched a squirrel, wrapped it in the cleanest, thickest T-shirt from the floor to prevent any seepage, and zipped it into the front of my backpack. For later. When I had privacy.

After dousing myself with hand sanitizer, I lingered in the dining room and studied their living quarters more closely, finding old magazines and a warped crossword puzzle book amid trash and clothes left where they fell. These people weren't neat freaks, that was for sure.

My dad would've hated their situation. *I* hated it. So, I set my backpack aside and sorted laundry into really dirty and only a little dirty piles. If Pollard was right about the stream in the forest then he could wash everyone's clothes and linens in the morning.

Pollard emerged from the kitchen. "Hey, don't do that." He pulled the clothes out of my arms and dumped them back on the floor. "You don't have to. You're our guest."

I didn't say that a proper host would offer their guest clean accommodations because that would've been rude. But I definitely thought it.

Hunny wandered over and jammed another mini chocolate donut in her already stuffed mouth. "What's for dinner?" she asked around a mouthful of pastry.

"Wild game." Pollard gave her a long look. "But first we're going to hold a memorial for our friend. You two can join us if you want."

Their friend was a stranger, but out of respect, I'd go along with them. "Yeah. Of course." I hadn't organized memorial services for anyone since the red plague. My mother had had a funeral two years ago, but that was different. I didn't know what people did when their friends and family died from zombie attacks. Or whether it helped ease the agony of losing them in the first place.

I wasn't sure Mom's funeral had helped me get over losing her. Yeah, I signed a card and added it to a bouquet of roses. I'd placed one of the white, colorless buds on top of her shiny coffin. I'd watched her sink into the earth. But she remained gone, and I missed her with a physical ache that never went away. Not completely.

Her funeral hadn't made her sudden death any easier to understand. I still didn't grasp that she could have been alive when I left for school one morning and dead before the last bell rang.

Or that Mason had been responsible.

Pollard passed into the kitchen, leaving Hunny and I alone in the dining room. But Hunny refused to be separated from her new protector, and she sprinted after him a moment later.

Maybe I should have held a memorial for my dad. Or Mason. But deep inside I wasn't ready to admit they were really and truly gone. It didn't matter that I hadn't seen or heard from them in two long weeks. They both could be out there somewhere barely hanging onto life the same way I was. If either of them had survived they must think I was dead, too. Unless I found them I wouldn't know for sure.

Pollard crowded the kitchen's rear doorway, waiting for me. Avoiding eye contact with Russell and Simone, I stepped into the warm, early evening air. Against the wall were a candle and a bunch of wildflowers, mostly weeds. Further down were another candle and a bunch of dry and crispy dandelions.

They'd done this before.

For Mom's funeral I'd worn an itchy black dress and pulled my hair into a neat and respectful bun at the back of my head. My dad hadn't let me wear jewelry. Too showy. And basic black flats were more appropriate, he'd said, than high heels. I'd agreed to whatever he said, too numb to protest.

"We'll miss you, Shelly," Pollard whispered, crouching to light the wick.

There had been candles in the chapel during my mom's funeral service. Lots and lots of golden candles. The back of my throat tickled, and I blinked rapidly. I wasn't sure what they represented, but whenever I thought of funerals I thought of those candles.

"I'm sorry I didn't protect you better," Russell said to the flickering orange flame. "I'm a crappy brother." His voice wobbled and he sniffed back tears. "But you were a good sister. A good little girl."

"Yes, she was," Simone agreed, looping an arm around Russell's shoulders.

The younger man embraced her hard.

"She's at peace now," Simone soothed.

Peace. They'd said that about my mom too. I swallowed thickly. Friends went out of their way to say things like, *She's with God,* or *She's with those who have gone before.* Or, my favorite, *She's living with the angels now.* Fricking angels.

Who cared about that? I wanted my mom *here*. The angels could fend for themselves.

A fat, salty tear spilled over my cheek.

Hunny grasped my hand firmly in hers, which only made the tears flow faster. Mason had been in lockup for Mom's funeral, but my dad had been there to comfort me. Actually, we'd comforted each other. Holding his hand had been like grasping a life preserver after falling into the sea. At one point during the service his hand had been the only thing keeping me from sinking into the abyss and floating away.

"Russell," Pollard said gently. "Do you want me to blow out the candle?"

"No." He sniffed again and broke free from Simone. "I'll do it." He dropped to his knees, sucked in a deep breath, and then blew out the candle.

Chapter Ten

After the memorial service for the girl I never even knew, I couldn't sit still. My fingers itching to *do* something, I organized the restaurant's dining room, which doubled as the group's bedroom and living quarters.

Hunny returned to the convenience store and gorged on more cookies and flavored water while Simone took Russell up to the roof for some privacy. Pollard busied himself cooking in the kitchen.

Whether Pollard appreciated my organizational efforts or not didn't bother me. I couldn't stay in a place, even for one night, that wasn't clean. My dad had drilled the merits of cleanliness into my head long before the spread of 212R.

I didn't waste any more time sorting laundry, but decided it was all dirty and piled it behind the hostess station. Either someone would wash it when I was gone, or not, but it was out of the way for the night. Then, after exploring the shadowy janitor's closet, I borrowed a broom and dustpan and swept the entire dining room. Nothing remained on the floor but microscopic dust particles, and I felt much safer.

I'd sprayed cleanser on the tabletops and was ready to wipe them down when Pollard emerged from the kitchen carrying a steaming pan of food.

He groaned when he realized what I'd done to his fortress. "You just can't help yourself, can you?"

That sounded like an insult. I rubbed hard at the plastic tabletop. "Cleanliness cuts down on disease. Everyone knows that." I shuffled on to the next table.

Pollard set dinner on the surface I'd just vacated. "Well, it looks better. I guess. But where are all our clothes?"

"Behind the counter." I moved on to the next table, and then the final one. "If you're serious about rebuilding civilization you need to think about keeping things organized." I glanced up. "Or are you more interested in a Neanderthal kind of world?"

"Very funny." But he wasn't mad. In fact, he closed the distance between us to poke me playfully under the ribs.

I giggled. Couldn't help it.

Simone stuttered to a stop under the archway between the convenience store and the

dining room. "Holy cow, girl. You work fast."
She grinned. "I can finally see the floor."

She turned on three battery-powered camping lanterns and the feeble light chased away the shadows.

"Hey," Russell complained. "Where's my stuff? You didn't throw away my board shorts, did you?"

"It's all behind the counter. Maybe you could wash the clothes in the morning," I proposed. "They stink."

"Gee, thanks," he said, laying on the sarcasm.

Once Russell confirmed his clothes hadn't been trashed, we all found a seat at a super-sized booth and helped ourselves to disposable plates.

Dinner wasn't simply wild game. No, Pollard had rolled little chunks of meat in a crushed cereal coating and fried them in a skillet over the fire. I didn't even care that I was eating squirrel. It was so delicious I wished I could eat more, however Pollard had seconds and then Hunny gobbled down the last pieces before anyone else could call them. But there were baked beans and canned spinach too, and I was full by the time I pushed back on my plate.

"So, Maya," Pollard said, wiping his fingers on a paper napkin. "You'll stay and help us?"

I inspected the faded, well-worn tabletop, tracing the geometric design in the plastic. Maybe, after I finished with my mission, but the cure had to come first. Even if this place was growing on me I couldn't let Pollard and his micro-community distract me from my plan. If I didn't find the cure and disseminate it, there wouldn't be a world to build.

"I can't." Not yet.

"I don't understand."

He didn't need to. My dad's elixir had nothing to do with the pretty-eyed college kid with bad aim.

"In the morning I'm leaving for my dad's lab in Raleigh."

There was a beat of silence as everyone stared at me with varying degrees of disbelief.

"Are you nuts?" Simone chided. "Have you been into the big cities? They're war zones. Packs of zombies. Cars and junk everywhere. Dead bodies in the streets. You can barely walk. I know. That's where I came from."

"It doesn't matter," I said. "I'm going."

"Why?" Pollard asked. "What's so important at this lab? A cure for the zombies?" He smirked, and Russell snickered.

My face overheated. "Yes," I said. "The last time I saw my dad he told me a cure exists. In his lab. He was waiting for approval to do human testing and then mass produce an antiserum, but then," I peered down at my plate, "things got really bad."

"There's a cure for 212R?" Simone asked, her irritation spiraling into disbelief.

"Things could go back to the way they were." Pollard glanced at me, and I recognized genuine hope in his eyes. He believed me. And he looked dangerously close to joining my mission.

I needed to nip that in the bud, quick. I was faster on my own, or I would be when my knee healed. A group would slow me down, need more provisions, and draw unwanted attention.

"I don't need you to go with me. I can do it on my own."

"You could." Pollard stood up. "Or we could stick together and be safe. Simone, how far away is Raleigh? On foot?"

Before she answered, Russell spoke up in a monotone. "I'm not going."

"Yes, you are," Pollard used his five-star-general tone again. "We all are."

"No," I said, my voice rising. "I'm going by myself."

Ignoring me, Russell jabbed a finger at Pollard. "I'm not going!"

"I'm not either," Hunny piped up. "I'm staying with you." She grasped Pollard's hand in both of hers and rested her head against his arm.

Hold on just a second. This was my idea. *Mine*, not theirs. I didn't need any interference. "Excuse me."

As if I hadn't spoken, Pollard focused on his friend. "You're upset about Shelly. I am too. But if we find this cure we can fix everything." His eyes brightened with a kind of zeal, and I regretted mentioning the cure at all.

Pollard wanted the old world back so badly he'd latched on to my plan with both hands. But he didn't know that the lab could've been destroyed weeks ago or overrun with Reds. The cure could have been moved. Even if it was there and viable, I still had to find specialists and equipment to analyze and reproduce it. Getting to my dad's lab wasn't even half the problem.

I took a breath to interject, but Russell spoke over me. "I'm waiting right here for the evacuation. End of discussion."

I forgot what I was going to say at the word *evacuation*. "Wait," I said. "What evacuation?"

In the early days I'd dreamed of Humvees rolling down my cul-de-sac and taking us survivors somewhere safe—a fantasyland with electricity and running water. My dad would be there. Maybe even Mason, if he'd fought his way out of juvenile detention, though that was a long shot.

But no one came to save me.

Russell pinned a pair of sad, shiny eyes on me. "The military is going to evacuate us. They dropped flyers." He rummaged around in a sack and came up with a piece of neon orange copy paper. "Here."

In bold, black print it proclaimed a military evacuation. "Paint the letters SOS on the roof of your building and wait inside. Helicopters will arrive and evacuate you to Camp Carson ASAP." At the bottom were a tiny date stamp and an official U.S. seal.

The government still existed? In Camp Carson there were survivors and soldiers and doctors? It sounded like a fairy tale come true.

"How did you get this?" My hand shook so bad the paper rattled.

"Helicopters dropped them all over this area."

"Have there been any helicopters since then?" I hadn't seen a plane in days and days.

"They're coming," Russell stressed. "It'll take time to find all the survivors, but they're coming."

I dug my song diary out of my backpack and flipped through it. On the last page I'd scratched tally marks to track my days in the bunker. Below those were notes on important days — the first day they broadcast a zombie on the news, the last day I saw my dad or had electricity. I counted backwards, using the date stamp on Russell's flyer.

"This is three weeks old," I told him. An eternity. "I don't think they're coming."

He snatched the flyer out of my hand, and then carefully smoothed out the wrinkles. "They're coming. They just need more time."

It was pointless to argue further with Russell. He was determined to stay, and I didn't need him, anyway. If Camp Carson existed I'd find it on my own. Later.

"Where is the lab?" Pollard asked as he attempted to extricate himself from Hunny's grasp.

I re-opened my book. In the front was an "if lost, contact" section and a long time ago I'd filled in my home address, my dad's work address, and our cell numbers. I knew how to drive there, but I'd have trouble finding detours through the city.

"Do you have a map?" I asked.

He chuckled. "Do I have a map." He jogged over to the convenience store section of the building and grabbed a folded paper map of the Raleigh-Durham area. "There's Raleigh." He dragged his finger from one point to another. "And here's us."

It looked like a long walk into downtown. Longer than I thought it would be.

"It's near William Peace University. Number 42 Vitriol Drive."

"I want to stay here with you." Hunny tugged on Pollard's army tee. "We'll be safe here."

Shushing Hunny, Pollard found the street on the map. "Right here." He jogged back into the store and returned with a pink highlighter. "This is our route." He drew a zigzag line down streets from our exit of the I–40 to the lab. "Simone, how long do you think it'll take?"

She studied the map for what felt like hours.

"When I left, there were fires and looting and zombies everywhere. All of MLK Jr. Boulevard, East Edenton, and New Bern Avenue were so packed with cars and trucks you couldn't cross them without climbing." All three streets were between Vitriol and us. "But maybe you can side-track and find an easier route."

My sore knee would be a huge problem if I had to scale clogged thoroughfares or hop over fences.

"It's almost ten miles," Simone added, "so on foot it would take about five hours, if we don't run into trouble."

"The dirt bikes would get us there a lot faster." Pollard frowned at all the intersecting streets.

On second thought, maybe having Pollard along wouldn't be such a bad thing.

"No, let's stay here," Hunny whined.

"You can stay here," I told her. "With Russell." They could barricade themselves in the truck stop and live quite happily for the one or two days we'd be gone. And I wouldn't be responsible for her anymore.

"Are *you* staying here?" she asked Pollard.

He glanced briefly in my direction. "What are you going to do with this medicine once you get it?"

"We have to take it to whoever is in charge. Camp Carson, I guess."

Russell perked up. "You want to drive to

Camp Carson?"

"Where is it?" I asked. I'd never heard of it so it couldn't be very near Raleigh.

"North of here. Outside Richmond, Virginia."

"Yeah," I mused. "I need to mass-produce the elixir. I need labs and chemists and all kinds of equipment. The army at Camp Carson can do it." Maybe.

But it was the best idea I had.

Everyone dispersed from the dining room. Pollard and Hunny cleaned up dinner while Russell slipped outside to smoke. I followed Simone behind the cash register.

Pretending to examine the little rack of energy shots beside the cup of novelty pens I asked, "Simone? You were in jail when Pollard found you, weren't you?"

Her eyebrows rose by increments. "He told you that?" She lifted a narrow bottle of amber whiskey from under the counter and snagged a decorative shot glass from the display behind her. "Yeah, I was in the drunk tank."

"All by yourself?" I asked.

She nodded slowly. "Thank God I was the only degenerate in there that night. And I don't even want to *think* about my final hours if Pollard hadn't found me."

Mason had a private room. Something about juveniles needing certain rights and privileges adult inmates didn't. Every night they locked him into a cell by himself.

"Could you have escaped on your own?" I asked. "If you had to?" Mason was smart and crafty and strong. Maybe, given the right motivation—death being a strong one—he could have gotten out of his cell, out of the prison, over the fence…

"No way." She swallowed a shot. "Those places are made to keep people in, even during the apocalypse."

Maybe Mason hadn't escaped. Maybe Ben had stolen his photo after the plague swept through. Maybe his having my picture didn't mean anything.

I stared at the lotto advertisement on the counter, not really seeing it. "My brother was locked up in Raleigh when the world fell," I admitted. "I was just hoping."

"Sorry, darlin'." Her voice got a little softer around the edges, a little kinder. "I wouldn't hold out too much hope."

"I know he's dead." It was like the words whooshed out of me, it was such a relief to say them out loud and truly believe them. "He would've come home by now. He wasn't that far away." I blinked back tears and shrugged at Simone.

If I had been able to limp from my home halfway to Raleigh in about a day, it shouldn't take two weeks for him to find me. It wasn't like I was hiding from him. After everything he'd done to me and Mom and our whole family, it still would've been a relief to see him again. To know I wasn't alone.

"Here." Simone grabbed another shot glass and poured whiskey into both. "To your brother. May he rest in peace." She nudged the drink toward me.

I accepted the glass, sniffed it, and winced at the strong scent. Like gasoline. Holding my breath, I downed the shot. Alcohol burned my throat, and I choked.

"It's awful," I exclaimed, my voice hoarse.

Simone smirked. "Isn't it?" She poured a second shot and tossed it back.

"Maya?" Pollard appeared around the corner. He frowned at the signs of our alcohol consumption but didn't mention it. "I set out extra pillows and blankets for you on the bench next to Hunny's."

"Oh." I glanced at Simone, but she got suddenly busy putting the shot glasses away. "Thank you."

He motioned me across the room to where he'd made my pallet. "Do you need anything else before bed?"

I shook my head at the puffy mound of bedding. "It looks nice." It looked suffocating. I'd go along with the plan until after light's out, but there was no way I was sleeping out there in the middle of strangers all night.

"Thanks," I said and took my turn changing

into pajamas in the bathroom. The whiskey made me thickheaded and a little clumsy, but by the time I settled onto my designated bench I felt almost normal again.

Hunny was the first to fall asleep, and Pollard was the last. I lay on my bench, an overstuffed winter jacket for a pillow, listening to each person's distinctive breath. Hunny hardly made a sound, but Simone snored loudly. Russell's breath rumbled out of him. And I had a hard time hearing Pollard. Maybe he was just a quiet sleeper.

Confident everyone was out for the night, I collected the tightly wrapped raw squirrel from my pack and snuck out the front door into silvery moonlight.

In the cool evening air I limped awkwardly between gas pumps and abandoned semi-trucks by the light of a half moon, still not one hundred percent convinced this was a good idea. But after he'd followed me, protected me, and written me a message, I felt responsible.

He stood atop a grassy median strip, waiting for me. I felt more than saw his red eyes in the dark.

How would he look all cleaned up and with his hair combed? Nice, probably. Normal.

"Ben?" I didn't expect him to answer. The most he could do was moan. But he didn't even do that tonight.

I unwrapped the squirrel and for a moment

doubted the intelligence of holding food in front of a zombie's face. Even though he must have smelled it, he didn't react. His eyes remained fixed on me like he'd never seen a female before.

"Did you know my brother?" I asked. "Did you know Mason?"

Not a wince, not a smirk, not even an eye flutter. No response.

I don't know what I expected.

"If you're going to follow me," I said quietly, "then you need to eat." I tossed him the squirrel. It bounced off his chest and thumped against the ground at his feet. "I can get you more tomorrow. If you're still around. Pollard taught me snares."

He gave no indication he understood anything I said and completely ignored the squirrel.

I searched his blood-flecked face for the faintest hints of his humanity, but unsatisfied, my gaze wandered the length of him. The left side of his body was covered in a white mist of dried spray paint from his earlier message writing. He was taller than me, almost as tall as Pollard, but thin from the disease. He probably had brown hair, but it was so dirty it was now black. He wore no watch and no jewelry or anything else to give a hint to his personality or his life before the plague.

I had been lots of things six weeks ago—daughter, sister, student, songwriter. Now I was just a teenager with a limp and a sad song stuck in my head.

"I haven't been able to write a new song since the plague hit," I blurted out.

Ben shifted from one foot to the other.

"Before 212R I wrote everyday and played my guitar like it was attached to my chest. But now…" I scrubbed the sole of my cross trainer over the asphalt. "The last one I composed, in March or April I guess, was sad too, and I don't like sad songs."

The familiar melody flitted through my mind. I hummed a little, the fingers of my left hand curling into chords on the neck of an invisible guitar. "It's dark, and you're not home," I sang softly.

Ben was a kind audience. He didn't frown or shake his head. He didn't react at all. So I sang a little more.

"Why do you have to go? If I asked you to stay, would you stay?" I shrugged. "I told you it was depressing. I wish I could write something silly or funny or romantic, but all I hear anymore are elegies."

Ben watched me, his face blank. Was it possible he understood everything? That he knew what he wanted to say, he just couldn't make his mouth form the syllables?

"Ben?" I inched nearer. "If you can hear me, raise your hand." I held my breath, waiting, *waiting* for him to move his hand for me, to prove he was different from all the other voiceless, violent Reds.

But he didn't.

"Ben," I tried again. "Why are you following me?"

"Mmm," he moaned, his gaze traversing my face as if memorizing every curve and valley. "Mmmrr."

A chill arced up my spine and tiptoed across my neck. I was in an abandoned parking lot, in the dark, with a Red. All my dad's warnings echoed in my ears.

Ben was fast and strong. He'd taken out three zombies in moments and come away with hardly a scratch. If he'd wanted to, he could've been on me and tearing into my abdomen before I had a chance to scream for help. Not that Pollard could do much. By the time he found me I'd be dead from shock and blood loss.

An image of Ben hunched over my lifeless body flashed through my mind, as clear as if it had already happened. He had blood on his chin and up both arms to the elbows...

"I'm going back inside," I announced in a shaky voice. "Good night." I rushed toward the truck stop, only glancing over my shoulder when I'd passed the automobile barricade. Ben had his face buried in the squirrel's belly as he devoured its internal organs.

I didn't see Pollard in the shadows until I ran straight into him.

"You have a pet," he growled.

Chapter Eleven

I stuttered to a stop, my heart thrumming in fear.

Pollard had put his handgun back on his belt, and my skin prickled as if I stood too close to a fire.

He steadied me, but I jerked out of his hold. I couldn't be near a firearm while so much adrenalin ricocheted through me.

"Congratulations," he barked. "You've turned a human being into a German shepherd. I can put a leash on him for you, if you want. Did you ever see *The Walking Dead*?"

Very funny. "He's not a pet, and he's not dead."

"He might as well be. Everything that made him human got corrupted when he was infected." Pollard stared hard, forcing me to look away. "He's dangerous. And he'll kill you first chance he gets. Don't ever go near him again."

I bristled at his tone. I was not a little child. I'd been in charge of myself for the past two weeks, and truthfully a lot longer than that. I did not appreciate him ordering me around.

"It's none of your business," I snapped.

"Is that what happened to my squirrel? You gave it to *him*? Like he needs any help killing and feeding."

I tried to push past him into the dining room, but he blocked me.

"Do you know him?" Pollard asked again. "Yes or no?"

"No." It was possible we went to high school together, but I didn't remember him. Maybe he'd been a friend of my brother's. Or at least near enough to Mason to collect my note.

"I don't recognize him," I said.

"Then he's hunting you."

I glanced at Ben. He was done with the squirrel and had returned to staring at me, hands at his sides.

"He didn't hurt me," I said. "I don't think he will."

"I don't care if he can copy words onto asphalt. A monkey can do the same thing."

I wasn't sure about that.

"You have a gun, don't you?" He gestured to the handgun on his hip, as if I hadn't noticed it. "I have an extra one. If you ever get near him again you better have protection."

There was no way — not even a chance — that I'd carry a gun. I could barely look at them.

I touched the grip of my short sword. "I'll be

okay."

Pollard laughed. "With that butter knife? Where did you get it anyway?" Without asking, he pulled it from my belt and examined it. The sword was ridiculously small in his large hands.

"It was my dad's. He was a big *Lord of the Rings* fan. It's a replica of Sting."

"The sword the hobbit used?" He looked a little more impressed. "Does it glow?"

"Only around orcs." I smiled, but it felt strange, like I was out of practice. "I'm kidding," I added when it seemed as if Pollard might believe me.

"It's sharp," he said, "but it won't help against a zombie. They're too fast and too strong. Especially that one." He bobbed his head in Ben's direction. "You need a gun."

"No." I finally pushed past him. As far as I was concerned the conversation was over. "Good night."

It didn't matter what Pollard said, Ben was different than other Reds. I didn't know how, yet, but he was. If my dad had been there, he would've had all kinds of theories about adaptations and strains, and I hated that he wasn't there to examine Ben. If he'd been there, he would've known what was going on. The best I could do was observe and make semi-educated guesses.

If he stuck around long enough for me to study properly.

The thought of Ben disappearing during the night, maybe joining a pack and migrating to a larger city, caused an uncomfortable anxiety in my chest. I didn't want him to leave. Not yet. I wasn't finished with him.

I tripped over an empty soda bottle on my way across the room, but not even that or Pollard's and my hushed argument in the entryway had woken the others. They snored on, oblivious. But I was done pretending I could join them.

Sleeping out in the open surrounded by these people I'd just met had been a ruse. I could never rest comfortably on a bench in the dining room no matter how many pillows and blankets they offered me. It was too open, and the others were too close.

I considered the janitor's closet, but it stank of cleansers. I wasn't sure I could sleep in there without suffering a migraine.

In the kitchen, though, I found a walk-in freezer. It was a little bigger than my panic room, about sixty square feet compared to my fifty-square-foot remodeled pantry, but it reminded me a lot of home. Someone had stripped it of all edible material leaving empty shelves and barren crates ringing the perimeter. It smelled faintly of rotted food, but it was manageable.

I missed the familiar shapes of the stacks of canned goods, boxes of crackers, and powdered eggs, plus the bins of toiletries and kitchenware back home. There was no guitar in the corner. And my comfy little cot covered in thick blankets was long gone, but I liked it.

Without asking, I dragged bedding into the walk-in and made a nice little pallet in the center of the room. Beside my bed on the floor I arranged my backpack and sword.

"This is your bedroom, then?" Pollard stood in the doorway with a lit lantern in his hand.

"Yes." I didn't want to explain. He'd told me to make myself at home and I had.

"It'll get really dark with the door closed."

"I don't mind." Since the electricity had gone off I'd had to adjust to the dark. It didn't affect me the way it once had. "Good night."

He lingered another few awkward moments, but finally he answered, "Good night," and slipped back into the dining room with the others.

I paused on the threshold, listening.

"Where's Maya?" Hunny asked.

"She's making a bed in the kitchen. Why aren't you asleep?" Pollard responded.

"I'm scared. Can I sleep with Maya?"

"No," Pollard said. "She needs her space. Apparently."

"Can I sleep with you?"

"No," he said, sounding suddenly ten times more exhausted than he had a moment ago. "Get back to sleep. You don't want to be tired tomorrow."

I waited until I was sure no one was coming to find me and then I closed the door to the freezer, locking myself into the dark. Alone.

Chapter Twelve

"We don't need that much water."

"We'll die if we run out. What we don't need is more cookies."

Voices drifted through the walk-in freezer's metal walls and pushed the final remnants of a lilting and sad country song from my dreams. I rubbed at my eyes. I hadn't slept well at all, tossing and turning and suffering two separate nightmares about Ben. In one, I'd discovered him shot and bloody and dead by the gas pumps. In the other he'd attacked me with all the force and ferocity of a wild animal. Twice, I'd woken anxious and jumpy.

It turned out the walk-in was not a close substitute for my panic room at home. I missed the comforts and security I'd taken for granted.

By the time I found the source of the argument, Pollard, Simone, and Russell were all wrestling over a box of chocolate chip cookies, two gallons of water at their feet. No one seemed concerned that Hunny was stuffing handfuls of

Tootsie Rolls into her pants pockets. The little sneak just couldn't help herself.

And I was seriously reconsidering letting any of them in on my plan. They looked and sounded like a whole lot of trouble.

"Good morning," I grumbled, swinging my backpack at my side. "Is there enough water to wash up?"

The walk-in hadn't only been pitch black at night, but it had held all the warm air within its insulated walls. I'd sweated out any fluids I'd managed to drink yesterday and was now in serious need of a bath.

Simone's expression softened and she opened her mouth to answer, but Pollard spoke first. "Of course. Come on. I'll show you the bathrooms." He grabbed a jug of water off the floor and led the way into the dark hallway. "Do you need soap or a toothbrush? It's all here."

"Actually, anything you can find would be great." I didn't even have a comb.

Pollard brought me a ladies' toiletry kit in a zippered pouch off the shelf. It was like Christmas morning. I was that excited to see a toothbrush and toothpaste. Hygiene had gotten a lot tougher recently. I'd been able to continue brushing my teeth because it required such a small amount of water. But actual showers? Those weren't so easy to accomplish.

And forget about doing laundry. I'd begun wearing an outfit for a couple days in a row and then sealing it into a trash bag rather than waste buckets of water cleaning the clothes. So, getting a bath, even a modified one, was a special treat.

He set his lantern on the sink and shadows writhed across the walls and ceiling.

"Thanks," I said, suddenly shy. "I'll be out in a while."

I shut the door on him and unpacked my precious things and an empty canteen from my backpack. I flipped pages in my song diary, hastily scrawled lyrics flashing by in a rush. Everything from the first song I ever wrote, a love song called "A Night Out," to the last song I wrote before the red plague.

I cradled the iPad for a moment, remembering what life had been like the last time I turned it on and enjoyed its contents. I flipped open the cover, but it didn't power on. It hadn't been charged in weeks. Inside its tiny parts lay so many things I cared about. Bands and music videos I loved, photographs, texts… Not that it did me any good.

I snapped the cover closed. It, along with its wall charger and ear buds, went back into the very bottom of my pack. Then I piled the canteen on top of it.

I'd learned a long time ago how to do an okay job of bathing with very little water. I stripped to my socks and scrubbed the small, soapy scrap of cloth over my body. Old skin and dried sweat sloughed off, and I felt a thousand percent better immediately. Then I washed the soap off with a clean, wet washcloth.

My hair, though, required more finesse. I bent over the sink, flipped my dark, glossy hair up over my face, and wet it with water from the jug. I lathered up with the shampoo and then rinsed it clean. The same with the conditioner.

During the first few days after my dad didn't come home I'd wasted a lot of water bathing my entire body. Another rookie mistake.

I'd learned to wash up with no more than a couple quarts and a washcloth.

I emerged twenty minutes later from the truck stop bathroom fresh and clear-headed.

While Russell continued to argue over supplies, I pulled Hunny onto my lap.

"I'm going to brush your hair," I pronounced with confidence, producing a small brush I'd gotten out of the convenience store.

She squirmed like a wet eel. "No."

I held on tight. "You have to. It's a bird's nest."

"No!" She kicked me in the left shin. Hard. "It hurts!"

"Okay, okay." I squeezed her around the middle to get her attention and felt every one of her ribs like piano keys through her shirt. "Let's make a deal."

She ceased squirming. "What kind of deal?"

"You let me brush your hair and I'll let you do something you want." Bribery had always worked with my brother.

"Like what?" She shifted around until she sat comfortably on my lap, but I kept my arms around her in case she bolted.

"What do you want? Let's negotiate."

"I want to go to a toy store."

The only one I knew of was near my house, but in the opposite direction we were traveling. We'd have to find another one along the way. But that wasn't too big a problem. After Hunny's thieving incident I wanted to get her something she could call her own. Something she didn't have to steal and hide under her shirt.

"Does this mean you're coming with us?" I asked.

"If Pollard's going, I'm going, too."

I sighed. "Okay, I agree to your terms. But, out of curiosity, what do you want at the toy store?"

"A Saddle Club Molly doll," she said very fast. "She's my favorite."

That sounded fancy. And fancy toys were often big. "You know you can only pick out what you can carry, right?" Our backpacks were already stuffed with essentials. No one would be able to lug a bunch of dolls, too.

"She's this big." Hunny spread her hands about eighteen inches wide. "And I'll carry her in one of those," she patted her chest, "baby carriers."

"Oh." That might work. "Okay. It's a deal."

It would mean time wasted picking around a probably already looted toy store, but if it would make Hunny happy and get her to brush her hair, then it would be worth it.

"But," I added, while we were still negotiating, "you have to brush your hair every day. And your teeth, too. We're not animals."

"Ugh. Fine." She heaved a sigh and went limp in my arms. "Go slow."

Willa may have been caring for Hunny, but she obviously hadn't made grooming a priority. It must have been weeks since Hunny's blonde curls had seen a brush. Several dreadlocks had formed in the back and I was forced to cut them out. The rest I sectioned and tediously brushed from the bottom up until, finally, I could run the brush all the way through her soft, blonde curls without hitting any snags.

Pollard's question about us being sisters came back to me. I'd never had a sister. Just my brother. But I could tell right away having a little sister was a lot different than having a twin brother. This girl needed tons of supervision and attention, two things Mason had avoided. She was affectionate and, though I was out of practice being around kids, it felt nicer than my brother's standoffish behavior.

I moved my right hand in front of her face and finger-spelled, "D-o-n-e," just to keep her practicing.

She must have been reviewing her alphabet

signs because she immediately signed back, "*A-t l-a-s-t.*"

Pollard popped his head through the kitchen door. "You two ready for breakfast?"

Hunny stood and faced me, looking even younger and more fragile than she had before. She messed with her hair a little bit, fluffing it up in the back, and tucking the front behind her ears.

"Yeah, we're ready." I zipped the brush into my backpack as Hunny ambled through the dining room where Russell and Simone were setting the table for breakfast. I swung right and slipped into the kitchen with Pollard.

"Her hair looks nice," Pollard greeted from the makeshift stove, giving me a secret smile and a nod.

My insides warmed. "Thanks. What are you making?"

Pollard gestured for me to come closer to the pan of raccoon drippings, sugar, flour, diced peanuts, and herbs.

"That smells awesome," I gushed. Better than anything I'd eaten for breakfast in a long time. Then, seeing a moleskin notebook open on the sink beside him, I zeroed in on that. "You have a diary too?"

"Oh, uh—"

I picked it up before he snatched it away. "What do you write?" I flipped through a few pages covered in scribbly handwriting. Random words caught my eye. Cumin. Sauté. Slice. "They're recipes."

"Yeah." He stirred his sauce with unwarranted attention. "I do all the cooking."

"That's cool." I used to hang out with other creative kids at my high school, poets and singers mostly, but never any wannabe chefs. "I'm impressed."

He frowned as if I'd said something shocking. "Really?"

"Definitely." I handed him his recipe book.

"I like taking the ingredients we can still find and making something that tastes good."

"I can't wait to try what you're making now," I admitted, cracking a wistful smile.

His blue eyes twinkled, making him look even more handsome. "You're so beautiful. You should smile more." Without warning, he pulled me off balance and planted a quick, soft kiss on my lips.

Before I could think what to do, he backed away.

I stumbled into the counter and an open sack of flour tumbled to the floor, dusting my sneakers white.

He'd kissed me. As if he owned me. As if I had no say in it at all.

He couldn't just go around kissing me without even asking.

"Do you always do whatever you want?" I said, hopping toward the door. "You shoot whoever you want. You kiss whoever you want."

His smile faded. "But I thought…"

I limped out of the kitchen as quickly as I was able.

When I next kissed a boy it would be with my participation, not some stolen, drive-by kiss. If Pollard didn't stop with this five-star-general routine I'd leave him and his whole group behind. Screw my sprained knee.

I flounced into a chair at the table beside Simone.

"Bad morning?" she guessed.

I grunted a noncommittal response.

Pollard took longer bringing our breakfast than it probably required, but when he did come in he carried a pan of stir-fried raccoon chunks in a sweet peanut sauce. I avoided eye contact as I helped myself to meat and a spoonful of canned peaches.

Though he was irritating me right then, Pollard was a talented chef. Breakfast tasted exactly like good Chinese food. He cared about cooking. That was obvious. I never could've made the same meal with only found ingredients and no electricity.

"We'll pack up and get out of here as soon as we clean the breakfast dishes," Pollard said, his head bowed. "The bikes are full of gas. I made sure this morning."

"Sounds good to me," I said around a

mouthful of fruit, keeping my eyes on my plate. "I'm ready." I'd carry supplies in my backpack, whatever they asked. I just wanted to *go*.

"Are you okay?" Simone laid her palm on Pollard's bare forearm. "You look upset. We don't have to do this, you know. You could stay here."

My gaze snapped up. Would he? Had my temper ruined my chance to drive into downtown?

"No." He kept his eyes lowered. "This could be our only chance to bring the old world back."

"Well, I'm staying here," Simone announced. "This place is too perfect to lose. I'll keep it safe for us. And if a military helicopter shows up to evacuate us I'll make them wait for you."

"You can't stay behind," Russell said, his voice echoing through the dining room. "Pollard, tell her. We have to stay together. Right?"

A little unfocused, Pollard said, "Maybe it would be safer for her to stay here where she can protect herself." He gave Simone a long look. "Are you sure about this? You don't have to."

"I'm sure." She nodded. "I feel safer here than out there." She gestured toward the boarded up windows.

That was fine with me. If I had to travel with a group I was glad it was a small one.

Everyone helped clear the table and Simone

washed the dishes with a bucket of recycled water. While she was busy in the kitchen, Pollard supervised packing supplies. In my backpack he assigned more water and a small first-aid kit. Hunny had to transport food and utensils. Pollard carried more water, guns, and ammo. Russell would lug toiletries and a tarp for sleeping under.

Russell bent over his pack, and as I neared I caught a whiff of stale cigarette smoke.

"Hi," I greeted, handing him a can of peas from the pile he was packing into his bag.

"Oh." He nodded uncertainly. "Hey."

"Have you ever been to Camp Carson?"

"No." He finished packing his bag and slipped it on. "Have you?"

I shook my head. I hadn't really been out of North Carolina except for a couple field trips and one family vacation to New York City. "What if there's no one there?" And we went all that way, wasted a lot of time and resources, for nothing?

"They'll be there," he assured, as if he was certain, when I knew he wasn't.

"Did you actually see a helicopter drop the flyer?" I asked.

"Uh." He fiddled with his belt buckle, jiggling the metal clasp. "I heard it. And when I ran outside there were flyers swirling all around the place. So…"

"Right." In other words, he'd exaggerated

the story. As far as I was concerned, the leaflet could just as easily have been a joke as an authentic public service announcement.

Russell turned dark, suspicious eyes on me. "Where did you come from?" he asked. "We've driven by that McDonald's a hundred times and never seen you before."

"I've been locked in my house all this time," I explained. "But I ran out of water." I studied him from the board shorts he was so concerned about to the shirt hanging loose on his narrow shoulders. "What's your story?"

He looked away, emotion clouding his eyes, and I remembered he'd lost his sister. "Our house got attacked. Mom didn't make it. But Shelly and I hid in the apartment above our garage for a long time." He adjusted the straps of his pack, loosening them until the bag rested on his hips. "It wasn't that bad. But we ran out of water, too." He nodded at me. "We were walking around, searching houses, and we hooked up with Pollard and his friends."

"There were more of you," I said, having already guessed as much.

"There was a guy and a girl." Russell scratched at his skull. "Alec and Desi."

"What is Pollard like?" I blurted out. I tasted him on my lips, still. Was I safe around him? Was Hunny?

"He's cool." Russell shrugged noncommittally. "He takes care of everybody.

And he's a really good cook."

"He's not violent?" I pressed. "He doesn't bully you guys?"

Speak of the devil. Pollard strolled out of the kitchen, spotted me talking to Russell, and silently passed us on his way into the dining room.

"No," Russell snapped. "Why would you say that? Because of yesterday?"

"He shot a little boy." It was kind of a big stumbling block for me. I didn't know if I could ever be friends with, let alone trust, a murderer.

Russell palmed his chest. "*I* shot that thing. Not Pollard." His face twisted into a mask of derision. "Pollard tried, but he can't hit anything he shoots at." He reached around to the small of his back and retrieved a snub-nosed handgun.

I instinctively put space between the weapon and myself.

"Don't feel bad for it," Russell said, replacing the gun in his waistband. "That thing would've killed you and Hunny and Pollard and me, too. It was a monster, not a little kid."

"You don't feel bad at all?" I couldn't help it. I did feel bad.

"No." He gave me a look like I was crazy. "I'm happy I killed it and saved all our lives." He turned away. "Jeez," he grumbled as he left. "So ungrateful."

I didn't understand our new world where every survivor was an unrepentant murderer.

Were we all killers under our polished, mannerly exteriors? Even fifteen-year-old kids?

Before we left the truck stop, maybe for good, I wandered the snack food aisles one last time. I hesitated to leave so much tempting food behind. No one would miss one bag of candy or a single juice drink.

Dad would tell me to make a healthy choice, dried fruit or something with whole grains. But I didn't want health food.

With so many yummy options in the convenience store, I chose an energy drink, teriyaki beef jerky, and a bag of butterscotch candies to suck on along the way. As I snuck a sugary disk into my mouth, Pollard appeared in my periphery. He was finished ordering everyone around and stood staring hazy-eyed at a display of postcards. He wore his holster and pistol on his hip.

"You all set?" he asked, keeping his distance. "You need anything else?"

"No." I hugged my loot to my chest.

He turned to go.

I blurted out, "Have you ever killed a Red?"

Pollard hesitated. "Personally?"

How else was there to kill a person? "What do you mean?"

"Well." He pretended to read the nutrition label on a box of ranch-flavored crackers. "I've been around when other people killed them. But I'm pretty sure my bullets never ended anyone's life."

"That's good," I said before I thought better of it.

His brows slashed downwards. "Why?"

"Maybe it's just me," I admitted, "but I don't want to kill any Reds. Not when there's a cure out there."

Pollard gave me an awkwardly long and searching look. Finally, he set the crackers on the shelf and gestured for me to head out. "Time to hit the road."

Russell unlocked the front door, and Hunny and I trekked outside into the warm, humid air.

"Wouldn't you rather stay here with Simone?" I asked Hunny, hoping my enthusiasm for the idea wasn't too obvious. "You could lounge around and eat junk food for two days. It'll be fun."

Hunny's gaze flickered over Pollard's tall form, and she heaved a sigh. "I'm going wherever he goes."

Her new defender lingered in the doorway to say good-bye to Simone. "Don't open the door to anyone." Pollard handed the woman a handgun and an extra clip. "Keep it loaded."

I wondered where they'd gotten their weapons, but life was so different now it was hard to know. Things were just lying on the ground, sitting in cars, or waiting to be liberated from dead people's homes.

Were survivors picking over my house? I

hadn't even shut the front door, let alone secured the place. I'd find out when I went back. After I found the cure.

"Check the snares every morning and you'll have fresh meat," he added. "You know how to skin and clean the squirrels and raccoons."

Pollard switched his backpack around so it hung against his chest, and then kick-started one of the Kawasakis. "Get on, Maya. We're wasting time."

I glanced at the second bike, but Russell and Hunny were already on it. It would only be more awkward to make Hunny switch seats with me. So, I swung a leg behind Pollard and clutched his shoulders. He waved once to Simone, and then took off across the parking lot, headed for the highway.

We sped past the spot I'd seen Ben the night before, but this morning there was no sign of him. Maybe the squirrel I'd fed him hadn't been enough to satisfy his zombified appetite. He could have headed south, back the way we'd come, to hunt. The idea that I might never see him again was discouraging. I wanted to see him again. His behavior had piqued my curiosity about the scope of symptoms of the 212R virus. I didn't want to lose the most human Red I'd come across.

Pollard drive right over Ben's message painted on the asphalt.

I shifted my rear end around to find a more

comfortable position and failed. The full cans of gas strapped to either side of our dirt bike put me in an unnatural position. And all that extra weight bogged down the Kawasakis. We made slow progress, rolling along only slightly faster than we could walk. But despite all the little hiccups, I was thrilled to be headed in the right direction. Finally. I was so close to validating my dad's life's work that I could taste it.

Chapter Thirteen

We chugged down the I–40, keeping to the very edge of the massive highway because it was impossible to cut through the mess of wrecked and abandoned vehicles. The shoulder lanes were the quickest and easiest to traverse. We drove slow enough that I didn't have to hold onto Pollard to stay astride, so I put my palms on my knees and absorbed all the changes to the city.

The end of the world was different than I'd expected. The new quiet, apart from the loss of so many people, was the most difficult thing to get used to. The wind made more noise than I remembered.

Over Pollard's shoulder the sad, quiet remains of our community zipped past. It was all just sitting there—houses, cars, clothes, cellphones, vacuum cleaners—untouched and unused. Because Reds didn't care about all the trappings of humanity they'd left behind when they'd been infected. And the citizens who'd lived there had either run away or gotten sick. Or been eaten alive by a zombie.

Perhaps eventually the infected would kill themselves off and reduce the entire world to one, massive ghost town.

The dirt bikes were a huge asset the first mile, or so, and then we hit a particularly awful section of the highway with forests on either side, no off-ramp in sight, and vehicles crammed in like Hot Wheels at the bottom of a toy chest.

"Guess we're walking from here," Pollard said.

"This is bull," Russell complained, pulling his bike over. "Let's turn around. We're not that far from the truck stop."

"We'll keep moving," Pollard said.

I walked ahead a little ways, but after sitting for so long my bad knee had frozen up, and it throbbed with every step. Thank goodness we didn't have to walk fast.

"Maya," Pollard called. "Get on my bike. I'll push you."

"I'm fine," I assured.

Russell passed me, propelling his Kawasaki by the handlebars through the mess of cars and debris, cutting high onto the grassy embankment. He grumbled something at me that sounded like *trouble*.

"Maya," Pollard said in his five-star-general voice. "You're injured. Get on the bike."

I did not appreciate his tone. He thought he

could order everyone around? Well, not me. I didn't need a guardian or a protector.

After he'd put his mouth on mine, a little space was appreciated.

I was much more concerned with why Ben hadn't killed me when he had the chance. Or how I was going to synthesize my dad's 212R elixir. Or where I was going to find enough fresh water to last the week. Boyfriends and dates and hooking up all seemed relics of an ancient civilization.

Kissing strange boys was way, way low on my priority list. Even if we might be the last plague survivors on the planet.

"I said I'm fine." I walked gingerly around a baby blue Mustang, using the hood as a crutch.

Pollard stepped into my path. "That was rude. I'm sorry," he said, offering his arm for me to lean on.

It hung there.

Waiting for me to make a decision.

"Will you please get on the bike?" he pressed.

The stubborn part of me wanted to say, *No*, but the ache in my knee had me nodding.

I gripped his arm and climbed astride the dirt bike. Pollard shoved the Kawasaki forward by the handlebars. But I hadn't considered, to reach the handles he had to lean in close. His chest pressed against my left shoulder, warm and solid.

I felt every breath he took.

"Maya!" Hunny shouted in a startlingly high-pitched voice.

I nearly fell off the bike. "Good Lord," I complained, palming the gas tank to stay upright. "What's wrong?"

"Look!" At the next off-ramp were signs for a fried chicken restaurant, a discount store, and a gas station. Oh. And a toy store.

I didn't want to stop. Besides the fact that the strip mall could be infested with Reds, walking up there, finding her pony dolls, and getting back on the road would waste precious time. A detour like that could set us back hours.

But I'd promised. "We need to make a pit stop," I announced.

Pollard squinted at the signs. "Why? There could be a thousand Reds over there. We should stick to the plan."

"Yeah," Russell piped up. "Stick to the plan."

"I'm not asking for permission," I said. "You can wait for us, or you can leave without us."

Pollard gave me a frustrated look. "You better have a good reason for this. Like, life altering."

Sort of. Hunny's life would be altered because she'd be a lot happier. But I didn't think he'd appreciate that, so I didn't say anything.

The boys rolled the bikes along the grassy edge of the highway and at the next off-ramp parked them in front of an overturned semi-truck.

"Okay," Pollard began, still in commander mode. "We're ninjas, you hear me? No unnecessary noises. No side trips. We go straight inside the toy store, get what you need, and come straight back. Everyone understand?"

My first few experiences with zombies had been accidental encounters. The Reds who'd chased me out of my neighborhood, little Jack, and the group Ben had saved us from. I'd never purposefully marched into a situation I knew would be full of killer zombies.

"And if there are Reds in the store, we're leaving without your stuff. No exceptions."

Then we better hope there weren't any toy-loving Reds hanging around. Hunny would flip out if she couldn't get her pony stuff. But chances were, the shop would be deserted. Humans were Reds' favorite food source and there weren't any people there.

Pollard took the lead and the rest of us trailed behind him in single file. Neither male pulled a gun, for which I was extremely grateful, and we quick-stepped it across what had once been a busy street and a parking lot. At the front doors of the toy store, Pollard scanned the interior. I stood back, controlling my breathing in order to hear the faintest sounds of movement.

Birds twittered as some trash blew under a

white Jeep.

"Hurry," he hissed, holding open the glass door for us. "No dawdling."

No problem.

Hunny went straight for the doll section, stumbling up and down aisles strewn with fallen merchandise. The store was a wreck. It had obviously been looted more than once. For bikes, bottles of soda, and baby wipes probably. There was more survival gear hidden within toy stores than I'd ever considered.

"It's not here," Hunny said, her voice overwhelming in the vast silence of the store. "They have Clara, but not Molly."

I hobbled to a stop beside her, kicking up dust and doll clothes. "So, take Clara. What's the difference?"

"Molly is my favorite."

I catalogued the brightly colored mess on the floor. "What does she look like?"

"She has blonde curls like me."

I searched the shelves for a blonde-haired Saddle Club doll. At the very top sat some more boxes. I climbed the shelf on my good leg and knocked them down.

"That's her!" Hunny tore the doll from her box and cuddled her like a long lost friend.

I got a warm sensation in the pit of my stomach. I hadn't been able to do a good deed for someone in weeks, and it felt nice.

"Thank you, Maya, thank you!" She gave me

a quick hug. Not an arm lock, but an honest-to-goodness, spontaneous embrace.

Yeah, a little sister would be a lot different than a twin brother.

I cleared my throat. "Good, then let's go."

"Wait." She squeezed the doll so tight Molly's head twisted at an unnatural angle. "The baby carrier. Remember?"

Couldn't we leave while we were ahead? "Where are they?"

Hunny found one on the next aisle made specially for dolls, put it around her narrow chest, and we caught up to Pollard as he ogled the train sets.

"We're ready to go," I said while Hunny fawned over her new friend, petting her hair and kissing the tip of her nose. At some point three decorative clips had appeared, as if by magic, on the left side of Hunny's head. And was she wearing lip-gloss? How had she had time to play dress up?

Not looking away from the electric train display, Pollard said, "I used to have one just like this."

I leaned in to get a better view through the Plexiglas. Once upon a time the model train had looped around an alpine village, through a mountain tunnel, and had probably made all kinds of sound and light effects on its way to the station.

"I think my brother did, too." Mason had

been obsessed with model trains for a while and he'd had a couple different sets, though I couldn't remember if he'd ever played with that specific one.

Pollard turned on me, leaning in way too close. "Promise me there's a cure at this lab." He furrowed his brow, his eyes reflecting fear and pain, which only further reminded me of my brother. Mason had often felt emotions more than most people did.

"Tell me we can fix all this. Tell me we can bring it all back."

I almost fell over Hunny who was sticking to me like glue. "That's what I'm trying to do."

We heard it at the same time. Footsteps and a low growl at the front of the store.

Russell appeared in the central aisle and sprinted past us. "Reds are coming through the front doors."

"Time's up." Pollard snatched Hunny off the ground, doll and all, and hugged her against his chest. We scampered into the rear storeroom. Dark shadows engulfed us, and something scurried among the bins and boxes.

Pollard outpaced Russell and I, even carrying Hunny, so he was the first to punch through the exit doors. Thirty seconds of running in the sweltering spring heat and I was sweating and breathless.

Pain knifed through my knee with every bouncing step, my sword banged into my thigh, and I quickly fell behind. Pollard and Hunny turned the corner, and I was briefly alone in the alley. I glanced back.

We were being followed.

And not by shuffling zombies from a horror flick. Oh, no. These people were as fast as we were, if not faster. And they were closing in on me.

I followed Pollard around the building. Now that the dirt bikes were in sight my confidence returned. One hundred meters. That was nothing. Bare-footed and blindfolded, I could sprint that distance faster than most people.

Pollard reached the dirt bikes first, set Hunny on the back of Russell's, and shouted for them to get going. He kick-started his Kawasaki, gray smoke spewing behind him. Despite regulating my breathing, the adrenalin and fear had me gasping for oxygen. I wasn't sure I was going to make it to Pollard in time.

The rear wheel spun out as he raced back for me. I pushed a little harder, too scared to look over my shoulder.

I didn't have to. I could hear their rapid footfalls on the pavement behind me.

Pollard skidded to a stop inches from my toes, and I jumped on the back of his bike.

"I knew this was a bad idea," he shouted.

He accelerated so fast I was forced to grab his shirt to remain astride. I finally chanced a look at the pack chasing us, and the nearest one's fingers came so close to my face I swore I smelled the rotten blood and flesh under her fingernails.

Pollard sped off across a patch of grass and over a curb. We weaved through parked cars and were soon out of sight of the toy store and the hungry Reds. My heart didn't slow down, though. I laid my cheek upon Pollard's shoulder blade and clenched my eyes closed. If he had been a little slower, or if my knee had buckled, or if Pollard's bike had stalled out…

At the next off-ramp, Russell pulled over and Pollard stopped behind him.

"Everyone okay?" Russell asked, eyeing each of us.

Maybe. Other than severe terror, I was all right. Both boys seemed fine, and Hunny was so happy with her new doll she didn't even enter the conversation.

"We're alive." Pollard gazed at the western horizon. "But it'll be dark in a couple hours."

"And the road's blocked," Russell added. "We're gonna have to walk again."

My pulse galloped through my chest and reverberated inside my skull like a hard-hitting bass drum. I'd almost died. And it had all happened so fast that processing it was next to impossible. One minute I'd been talking to Pollard and Hunny about model trains of all things and the next I was seconds from being tackled and eaten.

I shook my head to clear it, but hazy cobwebs remained.

I should have stayed in my panic room. I still would've died, but peacefully in my sleep from extreme dehydration, which sounded slightly better than being beaten and torn to pieces by zombies.

And then Russell's adolescent voice shattered the calm, and I tried to focus on the present.

"You guys want to play Twenty Questions?" he called as he pushed Hunny on his bike. "I'm bored."

I got my bearings and then pulled out our map and examined it. We still had a long way to go. "Dang it," I muttered.

"Go ahead," Pollard told him. "But keep your voice down."

"Okay." Russell paused. "I got it. I got something."

I wasn't in the mood to play games, but I asked, "Is it an animal?" simply to make the kid happy. My thoughts were still on that female zombie who'd almost had her hands on me.

"No," he answered. "Next."

"Is it a car?" Hunny asked.

"No."

Pollard turned his face toward mine. "You were pretty fast back there. Faster than I thought you'd be. Your leg must be feeling better."

The truth was, fear had overridden any pain

and I'd taken off at close to full speed. "I was on my high school's track team."

"Really?" He sounded impressed. "Were you any good?"

"I was always in the top three at meets." Back then my biggest concern had been what my hair looked like in the morning, or whether Cal was sneaking up behind me during lunch, but now running times—or hairstyles—didn't seem so cool.

"There was this one girl," I remembered. "Marcy. We used to pretend she had robot parts or something because no matter what distance she ran or whom she ran against she always came in first. She probably could have gone to the Olympics. She was that good." But there might never be another Olympics and Marcy was most likely dead. Dead or infected.

I couldn't stand the thought. "What about you?" I countered. "Did you play sports in high school?"

Pollard shrugged. "Football, but I was awful. I only played in three games my whole senior year."

"It was your dad's idea?" I guessed.

"How did you know?"

"I bet all you wanted to do was cook, right?"

He smiled. "Exactly."

"I write songs," I explained. "See, we both have secret obsessions."

"Will you sing me one?"

I pulled a face. "I don't sing, but I'll say it. If you want." When he nodded I recited something I'd written in my freshman year, long before the plague hit, "'Sunshine in my hair; sand between my toes. Must be summertime. School's a memory; longer days to play. Must be summertime.'"

"That's pretty," Pollard said.

Russell called out, "Aren't you going to guess anything?"

Without looking back, Pollard answered, "Is it the earth?"

"You are way off." Russell chuckled.

"Maya," Pollard said, his voice dropping. "How do you think you kept from getting infected?"

Easy. My dad taught me to be clean and safe. "I stayed in my house and sanitized everything I touched."

"I think we're immune," he said.

"To 212R?" I'd never considered immunity to be real. How could I determine, without a medical doctor and a lab, if I'd survived the Red virus because I was vigilant or because of a natural resistance?

"Have you read *The Stand* by Stephen King?" he asked. I shook my head, and he continued. "It's about a disease that wipes out more than ninety-nine percent of the world's population. But even one-hundredth of one percent of a billion people is one hundred thousand people. And there are more than a billion people in the world. That's us. And Russell and Hunny and Simone. The hundredth of a percent."

"Guys!" Russell snapped. "Did you hear me? I said you only have two more guesses."

"Uh." Pollard gave me half a smile before glancing over his shoulder. "Is it a vehicle?"

"No. Last question."

"Is it a toy?" Hunny blurted out.

"Come on," Russell complained. "It's Pollard's T-shirt. Jeez. I thought that would be easy."

Hunny wanted to play again, and she and Russell went back and forth, peppering each other with questions. I tried to tune them out as we made a snail's progress. At that point I could've gotten off the bike and walked faster than Pollard pushed it.

It wasn't his fault. The highway was a mess, and we were headed uphill for the next quarter mile or so. But I was still frustrated. Then Pollard opened his mouth and made it worse.

"We're not going to make it into downtown tonight," he said, eyeballing the high rises in the distance. "And there will be more zombies in the city. We should find a place to sleep around here while we still can."

Chapter Fourteen

"Are you sure?" Anxiety peaked inside me. I didn't want to spend another night without meeting my goal. "Can't we give it a try? We might make it downtown in the next couple hours, and then we could sleep in the lab."

Pollard shook his head. "It'll take longer than a couple hours on foot pushing the bikes. What if a Red corners us after dark? It's too dangerous. We'll sleep there." He pointed down the highway toward a shopping center at the next freeway exit.

I wanted to argue, but he was right. Damn it. No matter how much I needed to get to my dad's lab, we had to do it safely. What was the point of going through all this if I died before I found the cure?

We walked the bikes along the edge of the I–40, no one saying much of anything anymore. It was too hot and depressing to play games.

Pollard parked his Kawasaki on a strip of sandy earth between a thrift store and a car lot.

The front doors of the re-sell shop were smashed and twisted open. I stepped inside, avoiding glass and forgotten knick-knacks. This store had been looted too, but a lot of things remained, symbols of everything that had once been important. Sofas, dining sets, and framed art. No guitars, though. Not that I could have carried one on Pollard's dirt bike anyway.

The whole place smelled of shoes and sour Chinese food.

"Stay in sight and be quiet," Pollard ordered, giving a military hand signal for us to move inside.

Russell headed for the back wall, but I bee-lined for the clothes section. Scratching at my ribs, itchy with sweat, I searched for a pair of clean pants and a less constrictive tank top.

Still carrying her Saddle Club doll on her chest, Hunny ran straight for the gently used toy area. She got real quiet as she studied each colorful, plastic plaything.

"Pollard," Russell said. "I found camping gear, but there's only one tent. And it's small."

"Good." Pollard tested the weight of a cast iron skillet. "The ladies will have shelter tonight. You and I will rough it."

I chose a pair of dark blue jeans and held them to my hips. "Pick out new clothes," I told Hunny. "It's easier than doing laundry." There wasn't enough clean water to wash our bodies every day, let alone our clothes and bedding.

"Shoes, too."

She ignored me, so I chose khakis and T-shirts for her. I picked out fresh blue jeans, a white top, plus clean socks and underwear for myself. I stared longingly at the shorts, but if I didn't wear long pants my sword would cut my legs when I ran.

And then I chose a second outfit to pack into my bag for later. I was like a kid in a candy store with daddy's wallet. Though all the shopping should've made me happy, I couldn't manage it. I only needed new clothes because my entire life, the whole world, was thoroughly screwed.

"Cool, clothes." Pollard rummaged through the menswear rack across from the shirts I was sorting.

He picked up a pair of ski pants that had fallen on the ground. A giant rat cowered in fear at being discovered. I squealed, rising up on my tiptoes. The disgusting thing scurried for cover under a sofa bed.

A scream bubbled up from my chest. I tossed away the clothes in my arms and hobbled for the entrance. No way was I messing with rats. Spiders I could handle. Wild dogs I could reason with. But freaking rats? No, no, no.

I didn't stop fleeing until I stood in the bed of an abandoned pickup truck, panting for air and covered in goose bumps.

Pollard, Russell, and Hunny exited more calmly, each wearing new clothes and shoes.

"I think these are safe," Pollard said, dumping a load of clothing in the truck at my feet. Grinning, he asked, "You don't like mice?"

"That was a rat," I corrected, folding my arms. "And I don't know anyone who likes rats. They're filthy. And they bite." Plus their tails were creepy and they had black eyes.

Still smiling, Pollard lifted a lacy pink cocktail dress, the most hideous, backwoods prom dress ever made, from the pile.

"It's for you," he said.

I tried really hard not to make a face. "Thanks, but it's a little impractical."

"So?" He shook it out. "It's pretty."

If you say so. "Did you pick up the tank tops I found?" I sifted through the pile, less worried about vermin outside.

"Uh." He pushed aside a parka and a lone leather sandal. "I think so."

I pulled out the clothes I wanted to keep, plus a pair of cotton pajama bottoms.

Pollard glanced up the side of the thrift shop. "I think we can climb on the roof and spend the night. It'll be safe up there."

It was maybe the securest place I'd been since I'd left my house. If I weren't in such a hurry to get to Raleigh I wouldn't have minded living on a roof permanently. Or in a high-rise apartment complex.

It would be a lot of work, of course, clearing the infected out of a place like that and securing the ground floor to prevent future attacks. But if a multi-floor building could be controlled, it was the best possible shelter. And I could loot all the apartments for food, water, and toiletries. I got a warm, fuzzy feeling at the very idea of settling somewhere safe.

"I'll lift you girls up." Pollard stepped onto the cab of the truck and scrambled onto the roof in a pull-up fashion. A moment later, he reappeared over the side, both arms outstretched. "Toss up the bedding first. And then the supplies."

I did as he asked, passing him everything we'd need to spend the night and the next morning on a roof. Plus my private possessions.

I boosted Hunny up into his arms and then took both his hands in mine. He held firm, and I had no doubt he'd keep me from falling. Pollard was that kind of person. He'd protect and defend to his last breath. I used my feet to walk up, and he lifted me the rest of the way, but he wobbled off balance at the last second. We landed in a tangled heap on the gravel roof. I didn't move right away, feeling the hard planes and sharp angles of his body against mine.

His breath puffed against my cheek. "Did I hurt you?"

I swallowed, not sure how to delicately disentangle myself. "I don't think so."

With a slightly embarrassed look, and an arm locked around my ribs, he rose to his feet and steadied me. "I'll work on dinner," he said, snatching up two backpacks and marching away.

"Do you need any help?" I called.

Pollard didn't answer and I took that as a *yes*. So, I left Hunny and Russell to make the beds and crossed the roof to where Pollard was sorting his cooking supplies.

"Nothing fresh," I observed. After only two hot meals I was already spoiled again.

He gingerly set a sheathed knife atop a stainless steel frying pan. "There's not enough time to go hunting. And I don't want to risk it, anyway. I'm not familiar with this area."

"So, what's your plan?" If it wasn't eaten with a spoon from a tin can I didn't know how to make it.

"A stovetop casserole." He showed me a can of chicken chunks. "I'll mix a couple different things together."

I wasn't sure I'd ever had it before, but it sounded delicious.

"Will you open these and drain the liquid while I start the fire?" Pollard pushed a can opener and cans of chicken and black beans at me.

"Okay." I cranked off the lid of the can of black beans first. Careful not to spill anything, I carried it to the edge of the roof and tipped back my head, swallowing the sweet and salty fluid. After suffering a day and night from dehydration, it was too good to waste.

Movement at the far side of the parking lot caught my eye.

Ben had found me, and a thrill crackled along my nerve endings.

"Don't spill any," Pollard warned.

I startled, nearly dropping the whole can onto the pavement below. But I saved it at the last second and, not sure what to say, returned it to Pollard.

"Here you go." I picked up the next two cans and carried them to the roof's threshold.

Ben was on the move now, edging closer to our position, but he didn't seem to be in much of a hurry for a guy on the hunt. He must have run all day to keep up with us.

"You got those cans drained?" Pollard asked. "The pot's ready."

"Uh. One second." I opened and then swallowed the fluid from the last two cans while keeping an eye on Ben. He wasn't behaving aggressively. It was impossible for him to climb. And because he was harmless down there in the parking lot I didn't tell Pollard about our zombie tagalong. He'd go off again about Ben hunting me and how dangerous he was.

"I need those ingredients," Pollard said.

I scurried back across the roof.

Chapter Fifteen

We ate as a family would, as my family had before my mom died, gathered around Pollard's one pot meal of chicken, black beans, stewed tomatoes, and white rice seasoned with garlic and cumin. It was very good, made even better because Pollard had created it out of practically nothing, and it reminded me why shared meals had been so special. Before the red plague.

"Good food, man," Russell declared, patting his stomach after finishing two servings. "I need a smoke."

"I'm glad you liked it, but you can't disappear yet," Pollard said, scooping a last bite straight from the pan. "You're going to help me clean up."

The teen groaned and scrubbed at his stubbly red hair, but he picked up the dirty disposable plates and silverware, piled it onto the skillet, and followed Pollard to the makeshift kitchen.

"I like them," Hunny said, dropping her

head into my lap for a cuddle.

Finger-combing her delicate curls, I said, "Me too." They'd proven their trustworthiness. "You'll be happy living with them."

"*We'll* be happy." She glanced up at me. "Right, Maya?"

No. But she'd found stability and security with Pollard's group and I didn't want to scare her by telling her I was leaving first chance I got.

Though, who knew, would she even miss me when I left?

The day before, I'd been thrilled to discover a new group for Hunny, but it hadn't occurred to me then that she might bond to me. We'd only known each other for a day. The more time I spent with her, though, the more attached she became. *We* became.

I'd miss her when I left.

"Time to make camp." I urged her onto her feet.

The roof was flat and wide, broken only by air conditioning and heating ducts and some kind of electrical panel. I claimed a spot, as good as any, out in the open and prepared a bed.

I'd never slept communally before. This felt exposed and vulnerable.

I worried I wouldn't be able to fall asleep unless I was hemmed in by four walls. But this isolated spot away from everyone else at least gave me the illusion of solitude. I spread a thin blanket over the gritty roofing.

"Maya, sleep in the tent with Hunny." Pollard shook his head at my handiwork. "We got it for you."

"I like sleeping by myself." Being snuggled to death by Hunny for the next nine hours or so sounded like torture.

He groaned something unintelligible under his breath, and then declared to the whole roof, "Maya, you are the most stubborn person I've ever met. I'm trying to take care of you."

My cheeks flushed hot, and I watched him march across to the opposite side of the roof. I didn't get what the big deal was. Why did he care where I slept? I didn't have to sleep at all, if that were my choice. None of this was his business.

"Well," I returned loudly, "I never asked you to!"

"I *want* to," he shouted back. With quick, abrupt movements he laid out his blue tarp and piled it with jackets and bedding.

Hunny threw her arms around Pollard's waist and held on tight. "Please don't fight," she whined.

"Nobody's fighting." He massaged her narrow shoulders. "I'm just frustrated. Go make your bed in the tent."

I stared at Pollard's back as I attempted to form logical thoughts. I'd been taking care of myself for so long I wasn't sure why anyone would even want to worry about me anymore. I had things covered. But something had upset Pollard, which strangely upset me, too. Apart from the kissing snafu, he'd been generous and kind and I'd inadvertently irritated him.

I glanced at the spot I'd chosen for my bed. Maybe I could try something new. Hunny was a good cuddler, sort of like a breathing teddy bear.

"Come on, Hunny." I picked up my bedding and led her inside the green polyester dome. "I'll help you."

"Try to sleep." Pollard said. "We'll leave at first light." His mattress made of coats rustled as he settled upon it. "Wake me if you hear anything."

I created a pallet inside the tent with sweaters and some extra clothes. It wasn't so bad. It wasn't anything like a real bed in an actual house, but it was more comfortable than the walk-in had been the night before.

Hunny slid in beside me and wiggled around, catching me in the ribs with her elbow. Probably not on purpose.

And then, just as I'd feared, she threw an arm *and* a leg over my midsection. The temperature in the dome tent ticked up a few degrees. I lay very still to counteract her body heat and listened to all the sounds around us.

The birds must have settled down for the night, too, but several noisy cicadas buzzed in the trees below, reminding me not every living thing had been infected and gone mad. No footsteps, though. No doors opened or closed. No sound from the parking lot reached me at all.

Without any streetlights or house lights to ease us into night it got dark fast. Soon after the sun passed behind the horizon it was full dark.

I curled on my left, punched my jacket pillow, and then turned on my right side. Blowing hair from my eyes, I faced Hunny, who couldn't sleep either, apparently, and put my finger to my lips.

I signed, "*M-e p-e-e.*"

She frowned, and then figured out what I was communicating and nodded.

I dug the bag of beef jerky from my pack, attached my sword to my belt, and motioned for her to stay put. Where it was safe. She spread out onto my half of our pallet, essentially stealing my spot. I'd have to wrestle her out of it when I returned.

Before I descended I checked that Pollard and Russell were at least trying to fall asleep. All I could see in the moonlight were two shapes beneath the AC vent. But neither shifted when I zipped the tent closed.

I climbed down to ground level, falling the last five feet or so onto my rear end on the cab of the truck we'd used as a ladder.

"Maya?" Pollard called out. "Is that you?"

Crap. "I have to go pee," I said, hoping he'd allow me some privacy and not follow me into the parking lot. It wasn't that I was sneaking around, not exactly, but if Pollard saw Ben again he'd be pissed. He'd lecture me on carrying a gun. And I just wanted to get another look at Ben without making a big fuss about it.

Pollard didn't respond, and I pressed on with my plan.

It was dark and silent on the ground, nothing but the wind whistling through the buildings making any noise at all. I must have startled the cicadas with my tumble off the roof.

Before the virus, it had been a bright and busy shopping center. Now, it was another symbol of all the human race had achieved, and all we had lost.

Something moved on the opposite edge of the building. A shape appeared. A Red. I did what I wasn't supposed to. Alone and unarmed, I edged closer.

I reached the end of the sidewalk and circled Ben, giving him about fifteen feet of space, until I crunched through a patch of dry grass.

He plucked a small water bottle from his trouser pocket, showed it to me, and then rolled it across the grass. It bounced off my foot.

"Is that for me?" I picked it up. Still sealed. Clean and fresh. "That's funny because I brought you something, too." I tossed the packet of beef jerky like a Frisbee, and Ben caught it one-handed.

"You must be hungry," I whispered.

He sniffed the bag, but didn't open it.

I, however, twisted the cap off the bottle and took a long drink. "Thanks," I said, wiping water from my mouth with the back of my hand and then tucked the bottle under my arm for later.

"Do you remember music, Ben?" I glanced at the name embroidered on the breast of his dark navy work shirt. "Is that even your name?" It was always possible the shirt belonged to someone else.

But Reds didn't seem to care about fashion. It was more likely I'd see one wear the same outfit until it rotted off. So, Ben probably wasn't wearing found clothes. He'd been a mechanic once. Or a janitor, maybe. An appliance repairman?

His red eyes bored into me as he shuffled to see me more fully, the jerky pouch dangling from his left hand.

"I've been writing a new song. It's a little sad," I admitted. "But maybe it's appropriate. Maybe that's what I am. Depressed." I cleared my throat. "Way down here," I warbled, "I disappear. My heart hurts when you leave." I closed my eyes briefly. "I don't know. It needs work, obviously. But it's starting to come together. I just need a good chorus."

Exhaustion settled over me like wet clothes. I hadn't exactly been sleeping well the last couple nights and running from that toy store pack had drained me. I knelt in the grass, and then lay flat on my back.

Above me an endless ocean of stars stretched to the horizon. There hadn't been this many stars visible in the sky in a long, long time. It made me feel small and silly to worry so much about the virus when my whole world was a speck in a very big sky.

I heard a rustle and flinched, grabbing the hilt of my sword, my heart kicking into panic mode. But, no. Ben laid down, still keeping three yards between us, and turned his face toward me.

I had never seen an infected person behave so much like a human being.

"Who are you?" I marveled. "Where did you come from?"

His red eyes seemed to glow in the starlight.

"Why are you following—"

"Maya!" Pollard jogged over, his damned gun drawn. Russell was a step behind.

I hopped to my feet and put myself between them and Ben, partly because I didn't want them to shoot, but partly because I didn't want them to know I'd been lying in the grass with a zombie.

"It's okay," I said. "I'm okay."

A throaty growl sounded from behind me. The kind of warning rumble a big dog made.

"What is going on?" Russell demanded, an expression of utter disgust on his face. "That's a Red. Pollard, shoot that thing."

"No!" I held up both hands in a silent plea. "He's not hurting anyone. He's just listening to me talk."

"Are you hearing yourself right now?" When it became obvious Pollard wasn't going to shoot anyone, Russell stepped around him. "Zombies don't listen. They don't think. They kill people and eat their organs." His eyes got all shiny, and I suspected he was reminiscing about his little sister. She'd been murdered and probably devoured by zombies not that long ago. In front of him. "They're not your friends."

"He's not—"

"If it walks like a duck and eats human flesh like a duck… Do you get what I'm saying?"

I was sorry about his sister, but Ben hadn't been involved. He wasn't violent the same way other Reds were. He was different. "I should judge him on the actions of others? Now who's being a jerk?"

"Shut up, Russell." Pollard didn't holster his weapon, just slowly shook his head at me. "I thought something bad had happened. You were gone a long time."

"Forget this." Russell stomped away toward the truck we'd used to get on the roof and hoisted himself up.

I gave Pollard half a smile. "I found Ben. Or, rather, he found us." I glanced behind me. Ben was on his feet again. "Let's go back up top."

Reluctantly, Pollard came away with me.

What he thought of me and my zombie companion, I didn't know. Maybe that I was crazy. Sometimes everything felt a little crazy, me included.

"Maya," Pollard said under his breath. "Whatever you're doing, you have to stop."

I didn't pretend not to know what he meant. "Thank you for all your help," I said under my breath, "but it's none of your business." I wished I could flash back onto the roof.

I collected my water bottle and took a couple steps before I realized he wasn't beside me.

"It *is* my business." Pollard reached for my hand and twined his fingers with mine. He had nice hands. Strong. Kind of rough, but in a good way. "Because when he kills you, I've got to take care of it. If he doesn't kill all of us."

I didn't say what I was thinking. *Ben won't kill me*.

"Maya, I'm worried about you."

Our fingers were still linked. I hadn't even noticed.

"I'll be careful." I retrieved my hand and returned to the roof. Hunny was sitting in the tent, waiting for me. We laid down together and listened to Pollard settle into his pallet.

It wasn't easy falling asleep beside Hunny and her doll, and I woke feeling stiff and sweaty and slightly headachey. The morning sun and a faint breeze had turned the small dome tent into a convection oven and I scrambled into my new jeans and white top before emerging into the cooler air on the roof.

While Hunny slept on, snoring lightly and clutching her new doll to her bony chest, I stretched my tired and sore muscles. Pollard and Russell were already up and preparing to leave.

"Morning," I greeted.

Russell turned his back on me and lit up a cigarette on the far side of the roof.

Pollard smiled half-heartedly. "Did you sleep well?"

"No. You?"

"No."

I bent to zip the tent so Hunny would sleep a while longer, but her eyes popped open. "What's for breakfast? I'm hungry."

"Brush your teeth and hair first."

She grumbled about it, but we did our morning routine together.

Clean and groomed, we all sat around the pile of backpacks. Breakfast was a dry oatmeal bar from a box.

I observed Russell as I chewed. Last night had been awkward. His response to Ben, while understandable, was an overreaction as far as I was concerned. And a mediocre night's sleep hadn't appeased him in the least. The expression on his face told me he hated me, and Ben, too. In fact, I *disgusted* him.

Forcing down the last of my breakfast I excused myself and headed for the edge of the roof. Ben wasn't in the same place he'd been the night before. But he was still there, now closer to the buffet restaurant next door. There was so sign of the jerky.

Had he eaten it? Had he slept at all, or had he stood sentinel for ten hours straight? I wished I could study him more carefully and record his decidedly un-zombie behavior. If he had slept, what bed had he chosen? The cold, hard ground under a tree like an animal? Or had he found a more civilized shelter?

I was so wrapped up in my speculations I didn't notice Russell until he was about twenty feet away. He too was watching Ben. Then he drew his handgun from the small of his back and aimed it with both hands at the Red in the distance.

If Russell was a good shot he might actually hit Ben. My guts clenched inside a rusty vice. "What are you doing?" When he ignored me, I shouted for help.

Pollard reached Russell first and forced his arm down. "Stop it," he growled. "You're acting crazy."

Russell wrestled free of Pollard and backed away, the weapon still in his hand. "I'm crazy?" He laughed creepily. "*I'm* crazy?"

Hunny bolted and locked herself around Pollard's waist.

"There's a little girl up here," Pollard said, as if it weren't obvious. "Give me the gun."

"That's a zombie," Russell argued, pointing in Ben's direction. "How can you protect that thing? You know what they do!"

"He hasn't done anything," I said quietly, unable to hold my tongue any longer. "He's just standing there."

Russell turned bright, bloodshot eyes on me and I cringed. "My sister was *just standing there*," he mocked me, "and those zombies didn't care." He crept toward me. "Are you some kind of freak? You love zombies? *Zombies kill people!*"

Pollard stepped right in Russell's face, and his voice lowered. "Give me the gun. I'll give it back when you cool off. You're not thinking clearly."

Russell stared up at Pollard, his chest heaving. "You're going soft. You're gonna get us all killed because of *her*."

They had a sort of standoff as each tried to stare down the other. But in the end, Pollard won. Deflating like a balloon, Russell handed his weapon to the older male. Pollard immediately zipped it into his backpack along with his ammo.

Cigarettes and lighter in hand, Russell marched off to the far side of the roof to smoke and calm down. I hoped anyway.

The threat of violence quelled, I exhaled, not sure how long I'd been holding my breath.

Pollard gazed down into Hunny's eyes. "Don't be scared," he said, clapping her on the back.

"I thought he was going to shoot us," she said in a small voice.

"You know when something bad happens for no good reason and you can't do anything about it?" Pollard explained. "Well, it can make you really mad." He motioned toward Russell's back. "He's angry. But he'll eventually calm down. I won't let anyone hurt you."

I pretended to sort my gear, but I was too distracted and jumpy. Did I carry around an unnatural level of anger, just under the surface, because of what my brother did? And because I hadn't said anything to anyone after Mason threatened Mom? Or because my dad left me to go to work when he could have stayed?

Maybe.

But how did I get rid of it? How would Russell purge *his* fury?

"Let's pack up quick and get on the road," Pollard announced. "I've had enough of this place."

Maybe it was silly, but I topped off the bottle Ben had given me and tucked it into my backpack for later. Even though I already had a perfectly good canteen.

Within moments our camp was reduced to four backpacks, a doll in a baby carrier, and a rolled tent. Pollard used bungee cords to attach the tent to the exterior of my pack so it wouldn't go to waste. Everyone savored a final swig of clean water, and then we clamored off the roof and checked the gas levels in the dirt bikes.

After re-filling from the gas cans, Pollard caught me alone standing by the side of the building.

"He didn't mean it," Pollard began. "Russell. He's just…"

"Sad, I know." I didn't hold it against him. He seemed like an okay kid. I remembered what I'd been like right after my mother was killed, and I was no ray of sunshine, that's for sure.

Pollard leaned in, past an invisible line, and our eyes locked. I blinked first.

"And I'm sorry too about the, uh." He picked at the wall behind me, flaking off old paint and plaster.

The kiss.

I knew exactly what he was talking about. "It's okay," I assured. "I'm not mad." I'd been around him long enough to tell he wasn't a creep. In the kitchen he'd misread a signal or two.

I rubbed at my bottom lip.

"I just… I like you," he said.

I wiped my entire mouth and then stuffed my hands in my pockets. "Oh."

He eased off the wall and leaned even nearer, way into my personal space. "You're interesting and deep. I get that."

I briefly caught his eye. Maybe he did. "I like you, too," I said and then flushed red. "But," I added, and it was a big *but*, "I'm so focused on finding the cure," I mimed blinders on a horse, "I can't think about anything else."

Russell climbed onto his bike and assisted Hunny behind him. "What are we waiting for?" he shouted.

"Slow," Pollard whispered near my ear, gesturing for me to precede him. "We'll go slow."

The boys fired up the dirt bikes and, on the I–40, we passed the sprawling Atlantic Mills mega mall with its thirty-screen theater and one hundred fifty different shops, not including the hotel and restaurants ringing the property. Dozens of Reds roamed the parking lot, and every one of them looked up as we zoomed by.

As the sun beat down on my head and shoulders and the wind blew air, heavy with moisture, through my hair I thought of Ben, where he was, and what he was doing. I wished I could explain why Ben was so fascinating, since my interest in him was causing problems in the group. It was part him protecting us from a pack of Reds, part him copying my message on the parking lot, and part him going out of his way to bring me water. When he wasn't supposed to care about anyone anymore.

But if I actually found my dad's elixir and someone at Camp Carson mass produced it, the world was going to be a very different place that included both survivors and Reds. I had no clue how my dad's antiserum worked except that it counteracted and blocked the symptoms of 212R, but people like Ben might need extensive care. They and their rehabilitation would be part of our lives. Why not discover as much as I could about them now? Especially one who acted so human?

I doubted Pollard would see it that way. He was so focused on rebuilding what had once been he didn't recognize how much things had changed.

With the roar of the bike engine in my ears I didn't hear the pack of zombies until they stepped out from between two pickups, at least a dozen of them. Pollard tensed, the bike wobbled as if it too was unsure how to react.

Pollard punched up the throttle and plowed into the Reds, who were so spooked they only had time to reach out thin arms and bony fingers. The bike sluiced through the group, and then tipped and skidded away on its side. I fell, my head banged into the dry earth, and I tasted dirt. But I climbed to my feet as the group of frenzied zombies pulled down Russell's bike.

"Pollard," he howled. "My gun!"

Hunny leapt like a bunny and sprinted up the embankment.

I screamed her name, and she ran to me through a gap in the pack.

Russell, though, couldn't break free. He made a last, nonsensical squeal that sent shivers of horror zipping along my nerve endings. Those zombies pressed him into the ground and dug their fingers into him.

Everything went quiet for a single, heart-breaking moment.

"No, Russell!" Before I could stop him, Pollard tore his gun from his belt and shot at the mass of arms and legs, but all it did was draw the zombies' attention to us.

The instinct to flee was so strong the muscles in my calves and thighs clenched as if I crouched on the starting block of a one hundred meter sprint. I couldn't be around killer zombies and guns going off. I had to put distance between all this threat and me.

"We have to run!" I grabbed his free hand and pulled hard. "Pollard, we have to go. Now!" He resisted until I got in his face. "They'll kill us all."

I didn't want to leave him behind, but I would if I had to, in order to survive.

There was a whoosh and then a *boom* as Pollard's dirt bike caught a spark and all that gasoline exploded. Heat and fumes blew against my face, but we cut to the right and sprinted away from the Reds. Pollard and Hunny were faster, but my knee was healing and I kept up.

We ran off the freeway, circled a smashed delivery van, and broke into the first house we saw. Pollard barricaded the door, and we stood in the wrecked living room panting for air. It was even hotter inside than it was outside, and I scrubbed sweat from the back of my neck.

Hunny clung to Pollard's waist and whined, a kind of nonverbal plea to fate or God or whatever.

This wasn't good enough. I paced the room. I didn't need a hiding place. I needed to *run*.

"I can't stay here," I announced, my voice loud in the room crowded with overturned furniture and tossed cabinet drawers. "The Reds are too close." If they ran after us, which of course they would, they'd be at the door in moments. No wood or glass or stucco would keep them out for long.

Reds would tear a house to the foundation with their bare hands to eat prey cornered inside.

Pollard stomped across the room, groaning in pain. But not the physical kind. "Russell and Shelly." He slugged the wall and a spider web crack appeared in the plaster. "God, Russell and Shelly."

"Pollard," I said gently. We didn't have time to grieve. Later, sure, but not now.

"I'm such a failure," he shouted, and I cringed at his tone. "They trusted me to take care of them, and they're dead." He marched to the opposite wall and slammed his head against the drywall. "They were just kids."

"Pollard!"

A trickle of blood rolled down his brow.

"They trusted me. I'm a curse. I kill people."

"Pollard," Hunny screamed, wrapping her arms around him. "You have to take care of me."

He seemed to come back to himself. "I know," he said, his arms hanging limp at his sides. "I know."

"You're bleeding," I said, approaching slowly. I pulled my spare tank top from my pack and wiped his brow. *Thinking it's your fault*. That was kind of a specialty of mine. "You didn't do anything wrong."

He stared at me with glassy, unfocused eyes. "I'm not a soldier. I don't know what I'm doing," he whispered.

"It's okay. I don't either."

No one in this new world was stable. I thought of Ben following me into Raleigh and watching from afar. There would have to be new definitions for things like *normal* and *stable* and maybe even *human*.

Hunny's whining morphed into full on crying.

I didn't think Pollard would say any more, but finally, he said, "Do you know where we are? I don't want to go in the wrong direction."

Nodding, I pulled out the map and then passed my full canteen around. We weren't exactly on the move, yet, but at least we were talking about leaving.

"We're on Hammond," I said, studying the tiny street names. "We need to head north until we get to West Peace. Then we'll be really close."

I re-packed my bag and stood at the broken window, watching for the pack of Reds, or another one like it. Simone had said there were more of them in the cities, but this…

I'd never considered one of us would die for the cure.

I hung my head until my chin bumped my chest. Russell hadn't deserved that kind of end. We hadn't exactly been besties, but I'd never wished him dead.

Except he was.

To get the cure to 212R he'd given his life.

Hunny reared up in front of me, her eyes pink from crying, and shouted, "I hate you! It was your stupid idea to go to your stupid dead father's lab!" She clenched her fists, and her skinny body vibrated with rage.

I knew exactly how she felt.

It was easy for her to blame me for everything bad that had happened in the last few days. She was too young, too angry, and too sad to realize I felt the same way. We were both alone. Neither of us was living the life we'd envisioned. She could hate me if it made her feel better.

"I need to keep moving," I repeated. Staying there was suicidal. We'd all end up like Russell if we didn't hurry.

"Fine," Pollard snapped. "Let's go."

"Look for a car with the keys still in it," I

said. Speed was our best advantage.

"Okay." Pollard holstered his weapon and peeked out the front door. "All clear," he whispered. "Stay close."

Crouching in his shadow, Hunny and I followed him out. He headed for the street and a tangle of smashed automobiles, opening car doors with care. Down the block he found one with keys in the ignition, but its rear bumper was wedged too tightly between a pair of mini vans to drive.

We kept walking along Hammond Street, and then he found a truck with its nose on the sidewalk. The keys lay on the floorboards. Pollard tried it, and it started right up.

"Hop in," he said. "I don't know how close those Reds are."

I rolled down the window to release the cloying heat from the vehicle's interior and climbed into the passenger seat. But Hunny insisted on riding wild in the truck bed. There were no more traffic rules or highway patrol. Just the zombies and us. So, I didn't argue.

It almost felt like the old days. Me riding shotgun. I pictured this street the way it had probably looked a few months earlier. The abandoned cars and trash and debris were all gone. I saw normal, busy people driving to work or the mall or the beach. No one was sick with anything worse than a head cold. And no one had any idea of what was coming.

I closed my eyes and let the song knocking at my mind's side door to rush inside. *Way down here. I disappear. My heart hurts when you leave…* It wasn't the sort of song I wanted to be hung up on for days. But maybe if I wrote it, *purged it,* I could move forward and compose the kind of upbeat melody I loved.

"Which way?" Pollard asked, driving half in someone's front yard, half in the gutter.

I pulled out the map. "Go straight for a while. Then turn right on Vitriol."

He plowed over garbage cans and sideswiped a bus stop bench before stopping dead at a clogged intersection. Some panicked citizens had crammed their cars in until they'd created a wall of cold, twisted metal. With less than a meter to squeeze through, even up on the sidewalks, we were stuck.

"This all better be worth it," he said as we piled out of the truck and set out north on foot. "Don't tell me we went through all this for nothing, Maya."

Chapter Sixteen

Hammond Street was covered in random trash and debris, and here and there I saw a shoe or some jeans I was fairly certain covered a human body, but I didn't look too closely. I didn't want to see the remains of the people who'd once lived there. Watching Russell die had soured my insides so badly I didn't think I could handle any other evidence of zombie violence.

I just wanted to get to the lab, and then get out of the city.

We passed Hoke and Bragg Streets and a nail salon on the right, its facade untouched as if the owner had stepped out for a moment. Inside were wall shelves covered in colorful polishes that would never be enjoyed again.

Past the nail place was a Mexican fast food restaurant. A door banged, and we all jumped. I grabbed Hunny's sleeve and yanked her behind the nearest vehicle. Pollard, like a human shield, put himself between us and the noise.

A pack of zombies emerged from the small restaurant, stumbling and shuffling away from our hiding spot. There were two females and six males. One of the men wore a suit and tie.

My dad had worn suits to work every day. There were black ones and blue ones, and he chose the color by his mood each morning. His ties were mostly serious work types—solid red or black or navy. But he had one tie in his closet that was neon green with yellow SpongeBobs all over it. Every once in a while he would show up in the kitchen for breakfast wearing it, and we'd both laugh at how goofy he looked. But he'd say he was in a SpongeBob kind of mood, and he would go to work.

I missed that. Mornings with my dad, just talking about nothing while he poured cereal or packed a lunch. I missed seeing him smile. I missed his voice. I missed every little thing about him.

"They're gone," Pollard whispered. "If we go around, we should be okay."

I blinked away a veil of tears and pulled Hunny to her feet. She violently shrugged away from me and edged closer to Pollard. And for some reason the rebuff hurt more than it probably should have. Two days ago I couldn't wait to get away from Hunny. What did I care? She wasn't my sister. I'd only just met her.

I blamed Russell. His death had raked up old pain, whiffing it into a bright flame inside me. And maybe in her, too.

Sweat beaded upon my brow and I wiped it away before retrieving my canteen and taking a swig. But I was so upset my hands shook. I choked on the precious fluid, spewing it into the dirt and coughing raggedly.

Pollard tilted, trying to see into my eyes. "Are you okay?" he asked. "Did you get hurt when the bike crashed? How's your knee? Is it bothering you?"

"I'm fine," I hissed, wiping my mouth. The pain I felt had nothing to do with bumps and bruises.

Slowly, Pollard got moving again.

Tears burned very near the surface, but we were in the middle of a big city, a long way from anything safe or known or comfortable. I wanted to get to the lab before we ran into any other Reds.

Pollard halted without warning, and I stepped on his heels.

"Sorry," I said.

He shushed me. Then I saw what he saw. An old guy in a camouflage shirt and ball cap lounged in a folding chair on the roof of a small, boarded up house straight out of the nineteen fifties. He held a deer rifle to his right shoulder, its muzzle aimed at us.

My skin prickled as every nerve ending in my body stood at attention.

"Don't shoot!" Pollard called.

217

I walked in Pollard's shadow, my eyes on the asphalt and off the firearm. But I didn't have to see it to know it was there and my breath came quicker.

"Move it along," the guy shouted back. "I ain't got nothing for you."

Keeping an eye on the guy, Pollard led us down the sidewalk fronting his house. As we got closer I saw he'd wrapped the whole structure in yards and yards of razor wire, the kind on prison fences.

"Hey, Mister, have you heard of an evacuation?" Hunny shouted.

The barrel of his weapon moved fractionally in Hunny's direction. "I said, *move on.*"

"What about Camp Carson?" Hunny didn't know when to stop. Her big mouth was going to get us all in trouble. "Ever heard of that?"

"No one's coming to rescue you, princess," he jeered.

His bad attitude had no affect on Hunny. "Have you seen other survivors?"

Something behind us piqued the gunman's interest. I hadn't heard anyone following us…

And then I knew. No need to look at who'd caught his attention. I just *knew.*

It was like the whole world slowed to a crawl, and I could analyze every beat of time as it stretched around me.

"You got a Red on your six," the guy on the roof stated. He swiveled his gun away from us, and I took off running. I didn't care about my sprained knee, just dug in my toes and sprinted.

I didn't know what I would do when I got to Ben, anyway. Tackle him to the ground? Put myself between him and the rifle? I was a fast runner, but not even I could outrun a bullet.

It didn't matter. I was yards away when the gun went *bang*, Ben's body whipped around, and blood sprayed from his chest.

He fell.

I was too slow.

"Why?" I screamed at the man on the roof. "He wasn't hurting anyone!"

Pollard barreled into me, lifting me clear off my feet for a second. "Run, Maya, or he'll shoot us all."

"You some kind of zombie-loving freaks?" the man called.

Pollard half dragged, half carried me. "Run!"

"Ben!" I countered, fighting to stay. I couldn't leave him if he was hurt.

But Ben was on his feet and cradling his left arm.

Pollard pulled me, and I was afraid he would carry me away and leave Ben a target, again, for the gunman. I reached out, the way Ben had under the car days earlier, and grasped his arm. He didn't flinch away like I had.

We crossed the street together and blew through a hedge. Another shot sounded, and I instinctively ducked, but we turned the corner on a house and were out of sight of the gunman. For the moment.

"There!" Pollard pointed at something behind us, and Hunny scrambled toward it.

I didn't care what interested them, though. Ben was bleeding down his arm, staring at me with his crimson irises, seemingly indifferent to the blood loss, but I cared. A lot.

"Give me your shirt," I ordered Pollard.

Almost at the same time he shouted, "Hunny, see if the keys are in it. Get it started if you can."

But he heard my request because he handed me a wadded green T-shirt. I stretched it out, wrapped it around Ben's shoulder and under his arm where the bullet hole was, and tied the ends to stop the bleeding. Fresh, coppery blood stained both my hands.

My eyes met his and I froze, unaware of what was going on around me. For a split second there was no world, no Pollard, no Hunny, no 212R. Nothing but Ben. His navy work shirt was thick beneath my hand, and I felt the ridge of his bicep and the hard muscle across his chest. He was thin from the disease, but strong. He was taller than me, maybe as tall as six feet, and I had to lean my head back to see into his face.

Right there, high on his left cheek, he had a small, enigmatic scar.

I blinked and the world crowded back in. My bandage wouldn't last long, but to help it keep pressure I grabbed Ben's hand and smashed it against the knot.

He had strong hands. A working man's hands. I thought of my dad for a second and the way he always made me feel safe, even after our world had crumbled. Ben wasn't like that. His touch sent nervous electrical impulses up both arms, warning me to keep my distance.

"Time's up." Pollard bent and slung me over his shoulder, stealing me away.

I watched Ben get smaller. "Run," I told him. Maybe he understood me. I didn't know. "Run or he'll kill you."

I wanted to tell him to follow us to Raleigh, but Pollard wouldn't understand why I wanted a zombie to trail me. *I* didn't completely understand.

An engine started. Pollard opened the door of a vehicle.

"I'm going to get the cure," I told Ben. "Today. I'm going to fix everything."

Pollard set me inside an RV, squeezed in beside me, and closed the door with a resounding snap.

He took the wheel from Hunny, stomped on the gas, and got us out of there.

Hunny braced herself, but I lost my balance at the quick acceleration and fell flat on my belly. My knee pulsed with pain. I laid my face upon the warm, gritty carpet and closed my eyes.

In my mind I replayed those two seconds of horror. *Bang*, twist, blood spray. *Bang*, twist, blood spray.

I signed *s-a-d* against my thigh.

And then it wasn't Ben getting shot. It was mom.

I popped my eyes open, and my breathing revved into overdrive. I clutched my chest as breath whooshed in and out of me. I couldn't get it to slow down. Like a flip book all I could picture was Ben getting shot, and then my mom, and then Ben again. It wouldn't stop, and I thought my skin might crawl right off my bones.

The RV braked fast, and then Pollard hovered.

"Maya?" He laid a heavy hand on the back of my head. The contact made me jump. "What is it? Are you hit?"

I shook my head as I brought up both my palms, stained red with Ben's blood, and my breath got so out of control I started to feel light-headed.

"I left him," I gasped. "He's hurt. Oh, God. He's hurt and alone."

Why did I think I could do this? I wasn't a soldier, either. I wrote songs, not battle plans. I never should have left my panic room. Nothing but awful things had happened since venturing into the world. I'd messed up Pollard's stable little group. I'd separated him from Simone.

Russell was dead. And Ben was wounded.

Oh no. *Ben.*

"Maya," Pollard said, his voice rising. "I don't know what to do."

"He's hurt and alone," I repeated because it seemed to summarize every screwed up thought ping-ponging inside of my skull. "He's hurt and alone." *Just like Mom.*

"Maya!"

"It's a panic attack," Hunny spoke up from the passenger's seat. "Willa had one, like, every other day."

"A panic attack?" Pollard brushed dark hair from my face. "For what? *Ben?*"

Of course for Ben! "I just left him there bleeding. He could die." I turned my gaze on Pollard. "We have to go back."

I stood and reached for the door, but Pollard blocked me. "Maya, you're not going out there."

Two fat tears spilled down my cheeks. "He's bleeding and alone, Pollard. He wrote me a note. He brought me water."

"Okay, okay." He kept me away from the exit, though. "Let's think about this for a second. You saw the gunshot wound. It wasn't mortal, was it?"

There had been a lot of blood, but it was more of a flesh wound.

"And doesn't he always find you?" Pollard continued. "No matter where you go, doesn't he find you? He's a damned blood hound."

I bobbed my head. Whether I drove or walked or ran, he was always a step behind.

"He's not going to die," he pressed. "He's going to follow you downtown. Like he always does."

"But—" It was hard for me to accept what he was saying. It was as if my thoughts were on repeat.

"Let's do this." He glanced at the little girl in the front seat. "Hunny, we're going on the roof. Stand in front of the wheel and keep your foot on the gas pedal. If you see anyone approaching, press the gas pedal gently." He ruffled her blonde curls hair. "And when I say gently I mean *gently*."

"I will." Hunny started randomly pushing buttons on the radio until she triggered a CD and some George Jones song from another reality played from all the speakers. My whole body reacted. The tune sounded like the old world. Like home.

Rather than depress me it ignited a giddy memory of the way things used to be. Yeah, maybe life was currently rotten, but it had once been fun. And I had to believe it would be again.

"Come on." Pollard opened the ceiling vent, and then punched through the screening. He made a sling with his fingers and lifted me through the hole. As soon as I wiggled up, he followed.

Cars and junk lay scattered in every

direction. Off to the left I spotted a calico cat perched on the roof of a toolshed. On my right was a handmade sign that read, "God has forsaken us" nailed to a tree.

"I don't see him." I pivoted left, right, and then straight ahead.

"Come here." Pollard plopped onto the roof behind me and pulled me flush against his bare chest. "Give him a minute. He hasn't lost you, yet, has he?"

No, not since I'd found him standing alone in that grassy field behind my neighborhood.

Gravity had the RV rolling slowly down the cluttered lane. We passed the cowering kitty, and then Pollard knocked on the roof. "Hit the brakes, Hunny," he shouted.

Hunny did, and we slammed into each other. Pollard hugged me to keep me from falling, and even after I'd regained my balance, he kept his arms loosely around my waist.

The cat pricked up its ears and laid its tail flat against the shed's roof. I made a friendly clicking noise, but the sound of my voice spooked the kitty, and she streaked away between two houses.

"He'll be here," Pollard assured, his voice inches from my ear. His rough, blond whiskers scratched my cheek. "I have no doubt in my mind. I couldn't lose that dude if I tried." He chuckled and the sound vibrated through his chest and into me.

I wasn't so sure. After everything I'd been through, both before and after the red plague, I knew how quickly and easily a person could be lost. Permanently.

Russell had been consumed in minutes. What if a hungry pack found Ben, wounded and alone? Would he be able to fend them off?

I inhaled a deep breath. And then another. Pollard's warmth and strength seeped under my skin. All that adrenalin faded, and I wilted against him. I thanked God I'd found Pollard. I couldn't have gone through this alone.

I scanned the street, squinting to see even further. Minutes ticked by. We risked being attacked by a passing pack of Reds, and we were losing precious time. If we were going to find my dad's lab we had to hurry.

"Look." Pollard pointed down the street and to the left. "See him?"

I stood up so fast my shoulder clipped Pollard's chin, and his teeth clinked together. He groaned.

Then I spotted Ben. A lone Red in dark blue work clothes. He cradled his arm, but he was on his feet, and it only took him a moment to search out my position.

"See, he's fine." Pollard massaged his jaw. "You can relax." He urged me back through the roof vent and lowered me to the floor. Then he hopped down beside me, still cupping his chin.

"Did I hurt you?" I asked.

He shook his head. "Just bit my tongue."

I took in his bare chest. He'd donated his shirt to Ben's recovery because I'd asked him to. He'd looked after me, even when I fought him, and he'd helped me through the panic attack. I leaned up on tiptoe and kissed him.

"Thank you."

Pollard sucked in a ragged breath, and then yanked me flush against his chest. His arms circled me as he pressed his warm, soft mouth against my lips for a much different kind of kiss.

He held me gently, but his entire body, from his calves to his shoulder blades, went rigid.

Drawing away, I flushed and averted my gaze.

"You're welcome." He cleared his throat, and then pulled on a new shirt from his pack.

I slumped into the passenger seat as Pollard took the wheel from Hunny and drove the RV right through someone's front yard.

"You were really upset," he observed. "Are you sure it was only about Ben?"

I didn't know how he'd guessed, but I was ready to confess a part of the pain around my heart. The pain that was always there, like a plaster seal of grief and anger and regret.

I hadn't said the words in…

I couldn't remember the last time I'd said the words. Maybe I never had. I hadn't said them to Dad. He knew as well as I did what had happened. I hadn't told my friends. They read about it in the papers, and then Dad moved us away from my friends and teachers and neighbors.

"Uh." I swallowed past a dry, dry throat. "My mom was shot and killed two years ago." Pollard reached across the space separating us and grasped my hand, not caring about the zombie gore. He slid his fingers through mine, and Ben's blood squished against my palm.

"I'm sorry," he said with quiet sincerity.

I nodded, not sure what else to say.

"Guys," Hunny called from the kitchenette. "I think you just ran over a couch." Shaking her head at our lack of focus, she squirmed onto the extra soft captain's seat beside me and laid her head on my shoulder. So, I was forgiven.

Smirking, Pollard poked Hunny in the ribs, making her jump in glee.

I collected my paper map and scanned the happy looking green and blue blotches covered in zigzagging black lines.

"How much farther?" Pollard asked, gesturing to the map.

I squinted out the windshield to read the next street sign, and then estimated the distance. "About another mile. Stay on this street, and then turn right on Vitriol." Things were starting to look familiar. "Yeah. We're close."

Chapter Seventeen

"There it is!" I couldn't believe it. My dad's lab. Part of me had doubted I'd ever really see it again.

I hopped out before the tires had even stopped rolling and ran for the front doors. Someone or something had shattered the heavy glass. The speaker box on the wall beside a card reader where my dad had once slid his security badge hung from several black wires, smashed to pieces. With the doors swinging in the wind there wouldn't be survivors inside.

My heart dropped.

I stepped inside the foyer, searching for the faintest movement. Nothing. I'd had a crazy hope my father might be there, since it was the last place I knew he'd been before everything got really bad.

Dad wasn't there. The inside of the lab was a wasteland, just like the rest of the world. Gritty white dust puffed beneath my feet with every step across the empty reception area.

"You know where this cure is, right?" Pollard asked, leading Hunny out of the RV and keeping one hand on the butt of his holstered firearm.

I looked away, knowing seeing his weapon would mess with my emotions, and I needed a clear head. I had to find the elixir.

"Yeah." But that was ninety percent bluff. I'd never actually seen it. It might be there. Or it may have been shipped to a different lab at the last second. Or it might not exist at all, but be part of a fairy tale my dad had told me to keep my spirits up. Or an employee had taken it with them when they abandoned the building to the Reds.

But I knew where it *should* be.

I jogged across the marble-tiled foyer, kicking up more gray dust as I passed a wide reception desk and headed for the offices, storage rooms, and labs. Through a shatterproof glass slit in a security door I saw a long white hallway lined with identical doors.

The lab had great security. All its doors, even the interior ones, had been electronically sealed and had required a key card and a pass code to unlock. But after the power went out and any backup generators or reserve power was depleted, all the doors hung open.

I wondered for the bazillionth time what had happened to my dad. The last text my dad ever sent had been from this location on the day the lights went out. What happened after that? What prevented him from coming home? Was he wandering the streets of Raleigh, North Carolina, a mindless flesh-craving monster? Or had one killed him?

"Reds will come running," I warned. "Stay close. I know where they keep the important stuff." I ran straight ahead and made a sharp left at the intersecting hallways, but then stopped dead in my tracks.

A pack of Reds, five in all, were bent over a fresh kill, up to their elbows in blood. I didn't look too closely at the victim as I pulled my sword from my belt because on bring-your-daughter-to-work days I'd met a lot of Dad's co-workers. I didn't want to see any of them gutted.

Pollard rounded the corner, panting, "Maya, don't—" and then he spotted the pack. Hunny slammed into my back and squealed.

Pollard palmed his weapon as five pairs of red eyes found us, the body on the floor all but forgotten. Briefly, his eyes met mine, and I recognized the same panic swamping me.

"Run," he said. "I'll cover you two."

I couldn't run. They'd chase us like a pair of mice in a maze. I had no choice but to stand firm and fight.

My sword felt feather light in my hands as if it wouldn't pierce a piece of paper, let alone a human body. I tightened both fists around the hilt, but my arms shook so badly the tip of the short sword wobbled and swayed.

The Reds rushed us.

I shoved Hunny behind me and stuck my weapon out in front like a fireplace poker.

Pollard fired once, missed, and fired again. The sound and smell of gunfire jerked me into the present. The second shot hit a female Red, and she collapsed. But that only pissed off the other four. Pollard fired twice more, downed another, and I waved Sting, prepared to meet the remaining three with the point of my sword.

Someone ran past me, brushed me into the wall, and threw himself at the group.

"Ben," I breathed.

He swept the legs out from under one Red, and then tore into the zombies with teeth and nails. He was protecting us, giving us a few precious moments to escape. And all I could do was waste it standing there staring.

"Maya, go!" Pollard grabbed Hunny by the collar and shoved me down the hall.

I dodged the snarling, writhing mass of zombies, and yanked open the door to my dad's office. Pollard and Hunny crashed after me, and then I slammed it closed.

"Through here." I pushed into the sanitation room between Dad's office and the actual lab.

A few months earlier everyone who entered the main lab had to suit up. That's what my dad had called it. Clean scrubs, booties, gloves, mask, and snood cap. The works. That day, though, was a different story.

I bypassed the sinks and racks of supplies and let myself into the main lab. On the left were centrifuges, computer systems, microscopes, and all kinds of high-tech scientific equipment. On the right wall stood tall cases, some refrigerated, some locked, some not.

The problem was they'd already been ransacked. Someone had smashed all the glass cabinets and destroyed everything inside.

"Maya?"

Pollard stood over my shoulder. He saw what I saw, and he must have realized we'd come all that way for nothing.

"Are you serious?" Pollard lifted an electronic dispenser off the nearest counter and threw it against the wall. "It's not here? We came all the way down here and Russell gave his life for nothing?" Another heavy piece of equipment hit the wall, and then another.

This wasn't right. I hadn't traveled into the city of the dead for nothing. It had to be there.

My gaze traveled the mess of glass, scattered hypodermic needles, and dried goo. Not all the remaining vials were broken.

There. A few had rolled under the lip of a cupboard. I hopped over broken glass and dove for what could be the answer to my prayers. I belly-flopped and cupped the vial, squinting at the label. It didn't mean much.

"Aw, crap." Pollard stopped throwing

things. "Fire." I heard him and Hunny rush the door. "Maya, come on, the whole place is going to blow."

"Coming," I called, not moving. Pollard got Hunny out, but I couldn't leave until I made sense of the codes.

Strings of numbers and letters represented specific batches, dates, lab techs, whatever was important to log.

"212R," I whispered as flames spread across the central counter. It had the name of the zombie infection on its label. "A cure exists. I knew it."

Ben stumbled through the doorway, blood smeared across his face and staining the entire left side of his navy work shirt. At some point he'd lost the T-shirt bandage I'd made for him. He was breathing the hazy smoke through his mouth, and he looked more like a mindless, flesh-eating monster than ever before.

And he had me in his sights. He lunged for me, ripping the vial out of my hands, and then plucked a sterile hypodermic needle from the mess on the floor. He filled the needle from the vial before I fully understood his purpose.

"No, Ben." I tried to grab the needle and vial away, but he fought me. "We don't know the dosage. *Ben*. It could be a bad batch. It could be the red plague. It could kill you."

He jabbed the hypodermic into his neck and pushed the plunger.

"Ben!"

"Mmrrr." That funny growl of his.

I grabbed his collar in horror. "Ben?"

"Mmmaya." His eyes rolled up in his head, and he slumped, his face thunking against the tile floor.

The fire leapt across the central counter and attacked the broken vials spread around Ben and me. We had to move or we'd be toast. Literally.

"Ben!" I tugged on his shirt, but he was dead weight, and I only moved him a few inches toward the last corner of the room not on fire. I took a breath and pulled harder. I got his feet out of the fire when the wall behind me exploded. I threw myself over Ben to protect him from flying bits of brick and plaster.

Pollard hopped out of the cab of the RV, screaming at me through the giant hole he'd carved in the side of the lab. "Get in! Are you trying to kill yourself?"

"I'm not leaving without him."

Pollard swore. "This dude has been more trouble…" He slung Ben over his shoulder and then dumped him in the cramped interior of the vehicle. I knelt beside him, laying one hand to his chest. It was still wet with blood. His right forearm was chewed up from saving us from those Reds in the lab. But his heart was beating. The injection hadn't killed him outright.

"Don't touch him," Pollard barked. "He could be contagious." He grabbed my wrist and yanked.

"He took the antiserum," I shouted, jerking my hand free. "And I don't know whether he took too much. It could be poisoning him."

Pollard's face drained of color. "You found the cure?"

I shifted Ben's weight, bringing his head into my lap where I could better watch for symptoms of an overdose. "One vial. He injected the whole thing."

Swearing under his breath, Pollard got behind the wheel and reversed the nose out of the smoke-filled lab. "Everyone hold on tight. We're getting out of this hellhole and back to the truck stop."

He spun the wheel, stomped on the gas pedal, and we lurched over a curb. "Is he dying?" Pollard asked, catching my eye in the rearview mirror.

"He said my name." I still couldn't fathom it.

Pollard's brow creased. "Zombies don't talk."

"He injected himself with the cure, and he said my name." I bent over Ben, listening to him breathe, trying to determine with my limited medical knowledge the severity of his condition.

"Are you sure it wasn't a zombie moan? They do make noises."

"He said my name."

"What does that mean?" he asked.

"I don't know yet." I brushed a lock of filthy hair from Ben's brow.

A cure exists.

That's what my father told me.

If that vial was the last of it and Ben had just injected it into his body, then the answer to fixing the world coursed through his veins.

"You said my name," I whispered to Ben. "I know you did. Please wake up and say it again."

Excerpt from *Antidote* (Book 2):

Chapter One

"Maya!" Pollard made a hard right, the RV bounced over a median, and I held Ben even tighter. "He's a zombie. Back off."

"He injected the cure," I argued. "He's not a zombie anymore."

"You don't know that!"

"He said my name," I stated, still rocked by the memory of my name on his lips. I'd never heard a red-eyed infected person speak. No one had.

I felt the pulse at his throat and was rewarded with a strong thrumming against the pads of my fingers. Like plucking a bass guitar. His forehead, gritty beneath my palm, radiated heat. The fever had come on fast.

"Do we have Tylenol?" I called out. I didn't even possess a proper first-aid kit. And there were so many other things that could go wrong.

"Not that I know of," Pollard answered.

I wasn't even sure if a fever was normal in a person infected with 212R, the zombie virus. Maybe he'd had one all along.

"I can do this."

I had never done this. Over winter break I'd volunteered at St. Joseph's Hospital to make my dad, the chemist with two medical degrees, happy. I had alternated between stocking supplies my manager re-organized after I went home—which was awful—and trailing actual nurses as they did their work—which was awesome. One LPN used to narrate every single thing she did, from inserting IVs to checking blood pressures.

But none of it had prepared me for this.

"Where are we going?" I asked. If we found a hospital or a clinic I might be able to scrounge medical supplies.

"Away from this nightmare," Pollard said.

Away from the flaming remains of my dad's CDC lab. Away from anything he'd made or left behind. All that was left of his work coursed through Ben's veins and nowhere else.

As gently as possible, I unbuttoned the top two buttons on his shirt and peeled the dark navy fabric away from his skin to inspect the gunshot wound. A dime-sized hole, surrounded by angry swollen flesh, stared back at me.

I replaced his shirt and something like rough paper in his breast pocket, the one over his heart, stalled my fingers.

I pulled out a wallet-sized school photo and immediately dropped it.

"Crap." Fumbling, I picked it up off the RV's dirty linoleum floor and stared into my own face.

Mine.

To be certain, I flipped it over and my narrow, jagged signature adorned the back. Last Christmas I'd mailed the photo inside a care package to my brother Mason. It had been addressed to the Dogwood Juvenile Detention Center in Raleigh, North Carolina.

But if I'd mailed it to Mason, how had it ended up in Ben's shirt?

I stuffed the pic into my pocket. If Pollard or Hunny asked questions about it, I had no answers, yet.

I tested Ben's pulse again, this time the one at his wrist, just to be sure it still beat. But my touch jumpstarted a chain reaction. His fingers twitched, and then the tremors spread to his arms and legs.

"Oh, no," I cried out. His legs spasmed and his head knocked against my belly and thighs. Hard. "Ben? Can you hear me?"

Fear twisted my insides into origami as I held him through full body convulsions. Finally, his muscles quieted. I checked and re-checked his pulse.

"What's wrong?" Pollard shouted.

"The medicine made him sick." Understatement. More likely, it had poisoned him and his internal organs were failing.

"You're not going to die," I whispered as his seizure faded to a few quivers in his hands. Not with my father's only remaining elixir in his blood.

"Hang on to something," Pollard called.

About the Author

Anna Abner has been a writer for nearly her entire life, but some of her day jobs have included teaching, childcare, and real estate. She lives in North Carolina with her family and loves hearing from fans. Connect with Anna at www.annaabner.com.

Subscribe to Anna's monthly newsletter for sneak peeks, updates, and bonus material!

Other Books by Anna Abner

Spell of Summoning (The Dark Caster, Book 1)
Spell of Binding (The Dark Caster, Book 2)
Elixir (The Red Plague Trilogy, Book 1)
Antidote (The Red Plague Trilogy, Book 2)
Panacea (The Red Plague Trilogy, Book 3)

Made in the USA
San Bernardino, CA
17 January 2020

62977263R00149